THE
BOBBSEY TWINS
IN THE
COUNTRY

Dinner served in the dining car!

THE
BOBBSEY TWINS
IN THE
COUNTRY

by LAURA LEE HOPE

Book-of-the-Month Club
New York

The Bobbsey Twins in the Country was first published in 1907.

This edition was especially created in 2003 for Book-of-the-Month Club. This edition copyright © 2003 by Bookspan.

ISBN: 1-58288-070-0

Printed in the United States of America

CONTENTS

CONTENTS

CHAPTER 1

THE INVITATION

"THERE goes the bell! It's the letter carrier! Let me answer!" Freddie exclaimed.

"Oh, let me! It's my turn this week!" cried Flossie.

"But I see a blue envelope. That's from Aunt Sarah!" the brother cried.

Meanwhile both children, Freddie and Flossie, were making all possible efforts to reach the front door, which Freddie finally did by jumping over the little divan that stood in the way, it being sweeping day.

"I beat you," laughed the boy, while his sister stood back, acknowledging defeat.

"Well, Dinah had everything in the way, and anyhow, maybe it was your turn. Mother is in the sewing room, I guess!" Flossie concluded, and so the two started in search of the mother, with the welcome letter from Aunt Sarah tight in Freddie's chubby fist.

1

Freddie and Flossie were the younger of the two pairs of twins that belonged to the Bobbsey family. The little ones were four years old, both with light curls framing pretty dimpled faces, and both being just fat enough to be good-natured. The other twins, Nan and Bert, were eight years old, dark and handsome, and as like as "two peas" the neighbors used to say. Some people thought it strange there should be two pairs of twins in one house, but Nan said it was just like four-leaf clovers, that always grow in little patches by themselves.

This morning the letter from Aunt Sarah, always a welcome happening, was especially joyous.

"Do read it out loud!" pleaded Flossie, when the blue envelope had been opened in the sewing room by Mrs. Bobbsey.

"When can we go?" broke in Freddie, at a single hint that the missive contained an invitation to visit Meadow Brook, the home of Aunt Sarah in the country.

"Now be patient, children," the mother told them. "I'll read the invitation in just a minute," and she kept her eyes fastened on the blue paper in a way that even to Freddie and Flossie meant something very interesting.

"Aunt Sarah wants to know first how we all are."

"Oh, we're all well," Freddie interrupted, showing some impatience.

"Do listen, Freddie, or we won't hear," Flossie begged him, tugging at his elbow.

"Then she says," continued the mother, "that this is a beautiful summer at Meadow Brook."

"'Course it is. We know that!" broke in Freddie again.

"Freddie!" pleaded Flossie.

"And she asks how we would like to visit them this summer."

"Fine, like it—lovely!" the little boy almost shouted, losing track of words in his delight.

"Tell her we'll come, mamma," went on Freddie. "Do send a letter quick, won't you, mamma?"

"Freddie Bobbsey!" spoke up Flossie, in a little girl's way of showing indignation. "If you would only keep quiet we could hear about going, but—you always stop mamma. Please, mamma, read the rest," and the golden head was pressed against the mother's shoulder from the arm of the big rocking chair.

"Well I was only just saying—" pouted Freddie.

"Now listen, dear." The mother went on once more reading from the letter: "Aunt Sarah says Cousin Harry can hardly wait until vacation time to see Bert, and she also says, 'For myself I cannot wait to see the babies. I want to hear Freddie laugh, and I want to hear Flossie "say her piece," as she did last Christmas, then I just want to hug them both to death, and so does their Uncle Daniel.'"

"Good!—goody!" broke in the irrepressible Freddie again. "I'll just hug Aunt Sarah this way," and he fell on his mother's neck and squeezed until she cried for him to stop.

"I guess she'll like that," Freddie wound up, in real satisfaction at his hugging ability.

"Not if you spoil her hair," Flossie insisted, while the overcome mother tried to adjust herself generally.

"Is that all?" Flossie asked.

"No, there is a message for Bert and Nan too, but I must keep that for lunchtime. Nobody likes stale news," the mother replied.

"But can't we hear it when Bert and Nan come from school?" coaxed Flossie.

"Of course," the mother assured her. "But you must run out in the air now. We have taken such a long time to read the letter."

"Oh, aren't you glad!" exclaimed Flossie to her brother, as they ran along the stone wall that edged the pretty terrace in front of their home.

"Glad! I'm just—so glad—so glad—I could almost fly up in the air!" the boy managed to say in chunks, for he had never had much experience with words, a very few answering for all his needs.

The morning passed quickly to the little ones, for they had so much to think about now, and when the school children appeared around the corner Flossie and Freddie hurried to meet Nan and Bert, to tell them the news.

"We're going! We're going!" was about all Freddie could say.

"Oh, the letter came—from Aunt Sarah!" was Flossie's way of telling the news. But it was at the lunch table that Mrs. Bobbsey finished the letter.

" 'Tell Nan,' " she read, " 'that Aunt Sarah has a lot of new patches and tidies to show her, and tell her I have found a new kind of jumble chocolate that I am going to teach her to make.' There, daughter, you see," commented Mrs. Bobbsey, "Aunt Sarah has not forgotten what a good little baker you are."

"Chocolate jumble," remarked Bert, and smacked his lips. "Say, Nan, be sure to learn that. It sounds good," the brother declared.

Just then Dinah, the maid, brought in the chocolate, and the children tried to tell her about going to the country, but so many were talking at once that the good-natured housekeeper inter-rupted the confusion with a hearty laugh.

"Ha, ha, ha! And all of you are going to the country!"

"Yes, Dinah," Mrs. Bobbsey told her, "and just listen to what Aunt Sarah says about you," and once more the blue letter came out, while Mrs. Bobbsey read:

"'And be sure to bring dear old Dinah! We have plenty of room.'"

The prospects were indeed bright for a happy time in the country, and the Bobbseys never disappointed themselves when fun was within their reach.

CHAPTER 2

THE START

WITH so much to think about, the few weeks that were left between vacation and the country passed quickly for the Bobbseys. As told in my first book, "The Bobbsey Twins," this little family had a splendid home in Lakeport, where Mr. Bobbsey was a lumber merchant. The mother and father were both young themselves, and always took part in their children's joys and sorrows, for there were sorrows sometimes. Think of poor little Freddie getting shut up all alone in a big store with only a little black kitten, "Snoop," to keep him from being scared to death; that was told of in the first book, for Freddie went shopping one day with his mamma, and wandered off a little bit. Presently he found himself in the basement of the store; there he had so much trouble in getting out he fell asleep in the meantime. Then, when he awoke and it was all dark, and the great big janitor came to rescue him, oh!, Freddie thought the man

7

might even be a giant when he first heard the janitor's voice in the dark store.

Freddie often got in trouble, but like most good little boys he was always saved just at the right time, for they say good children have real angels watching over them. Nan, Bert, and Flossie all had plenty of exciting experiences too, as told in "The Bobbsey Twins," for among other neighbors there was Danny Rugg, a boy who always tried to make trouble for Bert, and sometimes almost succeeded in getting Bert into "hot water," as Dinah expressed it.

Of course Nan had her friends, as all big girls have, but Bert, her twin brother, was her dearest chum, just as Freddie was Flossie's.

"When we get to the country we will plant trees, go fishing, and pick blackberries," Nan said one day.

"Yes, and I'm going with Harry out exploring," Bert announced.

"I'm just going to plant things," prim little Flossie lisped. "I just love melons and ice cream and—"

"Ice cream! Can you really plant ice cream?" Freddie asked innocently, which made the others all laugh at Flossie's funny plans.

"I'm going to have chickens," Freddie told them. "I'm going to have one of those queer chicken coops that you shut up tight and when you open it it's just full of little 'kippies.'"

"Oh, an incubator, you mean," Nan explained. "That's a machine for raising chickens without any mother."

"But mine are going to have a mother," Freddie corrected, thinking how sad little chickens would be without a kind mamma like his own.

"But how can they have a mother where there isn't any for them?" Flossie asked, with a girl's queer way of reasoning.

"I'll get them one," Freddie protested. "I'll let Snoop be their mamma."

"A cat! The idea! Why, he would eat 'em all up," Flossie argued.

"Not if I whipped him once for doing it," the brother insisted. Then Nan and Bert began to tease him for whipping the kitten after the chickens had been "all eaten up."

So the merry days went on until at last vacation came!

"Just one more night," Nan told Flossie and Freddie when she prepared them for bed, to help her very busy mother. Bert assisted his father with the packing up, for the taking of a whole family to the country meant lots of clothes, besides some books and just a few toys. Then there was Bert's tool box—he knew he would need that at Meadow Brook.

The morning came at last, a beautiful bright day, a rare one for traveling, for a fine shower the evening before had washed and cooled things off splendidly.

"Now come, children," Mr. Bobbsey told the excited youngsters. "Keep track of your things. Sam will be ready in a few minutes, and then we must be off."

Promptly Sam pulled up to the door with the family carriage, and all hurried to get in.

"Oh, Snoop, Snoop!" cried Freddie. "He's in the library in the box! Dinah, get him quick, get him!" and Dinah ran back after the little kitten.

"Here you are, Freddie!" she gasped, out of breath from hurrying. "Don't go and forget poor Snoopy!" and she climbed in beside Sam.

Then they started.

"Oh, my stars!" yelled Dinah presently in distress. "Sam Johnson, you just turn that horse around quickly," and she jerked at the reins herself. "You hear, Sam? Quick, I tell you. Get back to that house. I forgot to bring—to bring my lunch basket!"

"Oh, never mind, Dinah," Mrs. Bobbsey interrupted. "We will have lunch on the train."

"But I couldn't leave that nice lunch I got ready for the children in between, Mrs. Bobbsey,"

Dinah urged. "I'll get it quick as a wink. Now, Sam, you rush in there quick, and fetch that red and white basket that smells like chicken!"

So the good-natured maid had her way, much to the delight of Bert and Freddie, who liked nothing so well as one of Dinah's homemade lunches.

The railroad station was reached without mishap, and while Mr. Bobbsey attended to getting the baskets checked at the little window in the big round office, the children sat about "exploring." Freddie hung back a little when a locomotive steamed up. He clung to his mother's skirt, yet wanted to see how the machine worked.

"That's the fireman," Bert told him, pointing to the man in the cab of the engine.

"Fireman!" Freddie repeated. "Not like our fireman. I wouldn't be that kind." He had always wanted to be a fireman who helps to put out fires.

"Oh, this is another kind," his father explained, just then coming up in readiness for the start.

"I guess Snoop's afraid," Freddie whispered to his mother, while he peeped into the little box where Snoop was peacefully purring. Glad of the excuse to get a little further away, Freddie ran back to where Dinah sat on a long shiny bench.

"Say, child," she began. "Do you hear that

music over there? Well, a big fat lady just jumped up and down on that machine and it starts up and plays 'Swanee River.'"

"That's a weighing machine," Nan said with a laugh. "You just put a penny in it and it tells you how much you weigh besides playing a tune."

"It does? Wonder if I have time to try it."

"Yes, come on," called Bert. "Father said we have plenty of time," and at the word Dinah set out to get weighed. She looked a little scared, as if it might "go off" first, but when she heard the soft strain of an old melody coming out she almost wanted to dance.

"Now, isn't that fine?" she exclaimed. "Wouldn't that be splendid in the kitchen to weigh the flour, Freddie?"

But even the interesting sights in the railroad station had to be given up now, for the porter swung open a big gate and called: "All aboard for Meadow Brook!" and the Bobbseys hurried off.

CHAPTER 3

SNOOP ON THE TRAIN

"Isn't Freddie good?" Flossie whispered to her mother, when she saw how beautiful the parlor car was, as if fearing her brother might forget his best manners in such a grand place.

Freddie and Bert sat near their father on the big soft revolving chairs in the Pullman car, while Nan and Flossie occupied the sofa at the end near their mother. The grandeur of the parlor car almost overcame Freddie, but he clung to Snoop in the pasteboard box and positively refused to let the kitten go into the baggage car. Dinah's lunch basket was so neatly done up the porter carried it very carefully to her seat when she entered the train, although lunch baskets are not often taken in as "Pullman car baggage."

"I'm going to let Snoop out!" whispered Freddie suddenly, and before anyone had a chance to stop him, the little black kitten jumped out of the box, and perched himself on the win-

13

dowsill to look out at the fine scenery.

"Oh!" exclaimed Mrs. Bobbsey, "the porter will put him off the train!" and she tried to catch the now happy little Snoop.

"No, he won't," Mr. Bobbsey assured her. "I will watch out for that."

"Here, Snoop," coaxed Nan, also alarmed. "Come, Snoop!"

But the kitten had been captive long enough to appreciate his liberty now, and so refused to be coaxed. Flossie came down between the velvet chairs very cautiously, but as soon as Snoop saw her arm stretch out for him, he just walked over the back of the highest seat and down into the lap of a sleeping lady!

"Oh, mercy me!" screamed the lady, as she awoke with Snoop's tail whisking over her face. "Goodness, gracious! What is that?" and before she had fully recovered from the shock she actually jumped up on the chair, like the funny pictures of a woman and a mouse.

The people around could not help laughing, but Freddie and the other Bobbseys were frightened.

"Oh, will they kill Snoop now?" Freddie almost cried. "Dinah, please help me get him!"

By this time the much scared lady had found out it was only a little kitten, and feeling very foolish she sat down and coaxed Snoop into her lap again. Mr. Bobbsey hurried to apologize.

"We'll have to put him back in the box," Mr. Bobbsey declared, but that was easier said than done, for no sooner would one of the Bobbseys approach the cat than Snoop would walk himself off. And not on the floor either, but up and down the velvet chairs, and in and out under the passengers' arms. Strange to say, not one of the people minded it, but all petted Snoop until, as Bert said, "He owned the car."

"That cat is the worst!" Dinah exclaimed. "It appears as if he is so stuck-up there isn't any place in this Pullman car good enough for him."

"Oh, the porter! The porter!" Bert cried. "He'll surely throw Snoop out the window."

"Snoop! Snoop!" the whole family called in chorus, but Snoop saw the porter himself and made up his mind the right thing to do under the circumstances would be to make friends.

"Cat?" exclaimed the porter. "Scat! Well, I declare! What do you think of that?"

Freddie felt as if he was going to die, he was so scared, and Flossie's tears ran down her cheeks.

"Will he eat him?" Freddie blubbered. Mr. Bobbsey, too, was a little alarmed and hurried to reach Snoop.

The porter stooped to catch the offending kitten, while Snoop walked right up to him, sniffed his uniform, and stepped upon the outstretched hand.

"Well, you are a nice little kitten," the porter admitted, fondling Snoop in spite of orders.

"Oh, please, Mr. Porter, give me my cat!" cried Freddie, breaking away from all restraint and reaching Snoop.

"Yours, is it? Well, I don't blame you, boy, for bringing that cat along. And say," and the porter leaned down to the frightened Freddie, "it's against orders, but I'd just like to take this kitten back in the kitchen and treat him, for he's—he's a star!" and he fondled Snoop closer.

"But I didn't know it was wrong, and I'll put him right back in the box," Freddie whimpered, not quite understanding the porter's intention.

"Well, say, son!" the porter exclaimed as Mr. Bobbsey came up. "What do you say if your papa lets you come back in the kitchen with me? Then you can see how I treat the kitty-cat!"

So Freddie started after the porter, who proudly carried Snoop, while Mr. Bobbsey brought up the rear. Everybody along the aisle wanted to pet Snoop, who, from being a little stowaway was now the hero of the occasion. More than once Freddie stumbled against the side of the big seats as the cars swung along like a reckless automobile, but each time his father caught him by the blouse and set him on his feet again, until at last, after passing through the big dining car, the kitchen was reached.

"What do you have there? Something for soup?" laughed the good-natured cook, who was really fond of cats and wouldn't harm one for the world.

Soon the situation was explained, and as the porters and others gathered around in admiration, Snoop drank soup like a gentleman, and then took two courses, one of fish and one of meat, in splendid traveler fashion.

"That's the way to drink soup on a fast train," laughed the porter. "You make sure of it that way, and save your clothes. Ha!" he laughed, remembering how many men have to have their good clothes cleaned of soup after a dinner on a train. Reluctantly the men gave Snoop back to Freddie, who, this time, to make sure of no further adventures, put the popular black kitten in his box in spite of protests from the admiring passengers.

"You have missed so much of the beautiful scenery," Nan told Freddie and her father when they joined the party again. "Just see those mountains over there," and then they sat at the broad windows gazing for a long time at the grand scenery as it seemed to rush by.

CHAPTER 4

A LONG RIDE

THE train was speeding along with that regular motion that puts many travelers to sleep, when Freddie curled himself on the sofa and went to sleep.

"Poor little chap!" Mr. Bobbsey remarked. "He is tired out, and he was so worried about Snoop!"

"I'm glad we were able to get this sofa. So many other people like a rest and there are only four sofas on each car," Mrs. Bobbsey explained to Dinah, who was now tucking Freddie in as if he were at home in his own cozy bed. The air cushion was blown up, and put under the yellow head and a shawl was carefully placed over him.

Flossie's pretty dimpled face was pressed close to the windowpane, admiring the big world that seemed to be running away from the train, and Bert found the observation end of the train very interesting.

"What a beautiful grove of white birch trees!"

Nan exclaimed, as the train swung into a ravine. "And see the soft ferns clinging about them. Mother, the ferns around the birch tree make me think of the fine lace about your throat!"

"Why, daughter, you seem to be quite poetical!" and the mother smiled, for indeed Nan had a very promising mind.

"What time will we get there, papa?" Bert asked, returning from the vestibule.

"In time for dinner Aunt Sarah said, that is if they keep dinner for us until one o'clock," answered the parent, as he consulted his watch.

"It seems as if we had been on the train all night," Flossie remarked.

"Well, we started early, dear," the mother assured the tired little girl. "Perhaps you would like one of Dinah's dainty sandwiches now?"

A light lunch was quickly decided on, and Dinah took Flossie and Nan to a little private room at one end of the train, Bert went with his father to the smoking room on the other end, while the mother remained to watch Freddie. The lunch was put up so that each small sandwich could be eaten without a crumb spilling, as the little squares were each wrapped separately in waxed paper.

There was a queer alcohol lamp in the ladies' room, and other handy contrivances for travelers, which amused Flossie and Nan.

"That's to heat milk for babies," Dinah told the girls, as she put the paper napkins carefully on their laps, and got each a nice drink of ice-water out of the cooler.

Meanwhile Bert was enjoying his lunch at the other end of the car, for children always get hungry when traveling, and meals on the train are only served at certain hours.

Soon the lunch was finished, and the Bobbseys felt much refreshed by it. Freddie still slept with Snoop's box close beside him, and Mrs. Bobbsey was reading a magazine.

"One hour more!" Bert announced, beginning to pick things up even that early.

"Now we better all close our eyes and rest, so that we will feel good when we get to Meadow Brook," Mrs. Bobbsey told them. It was no task to obey this suggestion, and the next thing the children knew, mother and father and Dinah were waking them up to get them ready to leave the train.

"Now, don't forget anything," Mr. Bobbsey cautioned the party, as hats and wraps were donned and parcels picked up.

Freddie was still very sleepy, and his papa had to carry him off, while the others, with some excitement, hurried after.

"Oh, Snoop, Snoop!" cried Freddie as, having reached the platform, they now saw the train start off. "I forgot Snoop! Get him quick!"

"That kitten again!" Dinah exclaimed, with some indignation. "He's more trouble than—than the whole family!"

In an instant the train had gotten up speed, and it seemed Snoop was gone this time sure.

"Snoop!" cried Freddie, in dismay.

Just then the kind porter who had befriended the cat before, appeared on the platform with the perforated box in his hand.

"I wanted to keep him," stammered the porter, "but I know the little boy would break his heart after him." And he threw the box to Mr. Bobbsey.

There was no time for words, but Mr. Bobbsey thrust a coin in the man's hand and all the members of the Bobbsey family looked their thanks.

"Well, I declare, you can't see anybody," called out a good-natured little lady, trying to surround them all at once.

"Aunt Sarah!" exclaimed the Bobbseys.

"And Uncle Dan!"

"And Harry!"

"Hello! How do? How are you? How be you?" and such kissing and handshaking had not for some time entertained the old agent at the Meadow Brook station.

"Here at last!" Uncle Daniel declared, grabbing up Freddie and giving him the kind of hug Freddie had intended giving Aunt Sarah.

The big wagon from the Bobbsey farm, with the seats running along each side, stood at the other side of the platform, and into this the Bobbseys were gathered, bag and baggage, not forgetting the little black cat.

"All aboard for Meadow Brook farm!" called Bert, as the wagon started off along the shady country road.

CHAPTER 5

MEADOW BROOK

"OH, how cool the trees are out here!" Flossie exclaimed, as the wagon rumbled along so close to the low trees that Bert could reach out and pick horse-chestnut blossoms.

"My, how sweet it is!" said Dinah, as she sniffed audibly, enjoying the freshness of the country.

Freddie was on the seat with Uncle Dan and had Snoop's box safe in his arms. He wanted to let the cat see along the road, but everybody protested.

"No more Snoop in this trip," laughed Mr. Bobbsey. "He has had all the fun he needs for today." So Freddie had to be content.

"Oh, do let me get out?" pleaded Nan presently. "See that field of orange lilies."

"Not now, dear," Aunt Sarah told her. "Dinner is spoiling for us, and we can often walk down here to get flowers."

"Oh, the cute little calf! Look!" Bert exclaimed

from his seat next to Harry, who had been telling his cousin of all the plans he had made for a jolly vacation.

"Look at the billy goat!" called Freddie.

"See, see, that big black chicken flying!" Flossie cried out excitedly.

"That's a hawk!" laughed Bert. "Maybe it's a chicken hawk."

"A children hawk!" Flossie exclaimed, missing the word. Then everybody laughed, and Flossie said maybe there were children hawks for bad girls and boys, anyway.

Aunt Sarah and Mrs. Bobbsey were chatting away like two schoolgirls, while Dinah and the children saw something new and interesting at every few paces old Billy, the horse, took.

"Hello there, neighbor," called a voice from the field at the side of the road. "My horse has fallen in the ditch, and I'll have to trouble you to help me."

"Certainly, certainly, Peter," answered Uncle Daniel, promptly jumping down, with Mr. Bobbsey, Bert, and Harry following. Aunt Sarah leaned over the seat and took the reins, but when she saw in what ditch the other horse had fallen she pulled Billy into the gutter.

"Poor Peter!" she exclaimed. "That's the second horse that fell in that ditch this week. And it's an awful job to get them out. I'll just wait to see if they need our Billy, and if not, we can drive on home, for Martha will be most crazy waiting with dinner."

Uncle Daniel, Mr. Bobbsey, and the boys hurried to where Peter Burns stood at the brink of one of those ditches that look like mud and turn out to be water.

"And that horse is a boarder too," Peter told them. "Last night we said he looked awful sad, but we didn't think he would commit suicide."

"Got plenty of blankets?" Uncle Daniel asked, pulling his coat off and preparing to help his neighbor, as all good people do in the country.

"Four of them, and these planks. But I couldn't get a man around. Lucky you happened by," Peter Burns answered.

All this time the horse in the ditch moaned as if in pain, but Peter said it was only because he couldn't get on his feet. Harry, being light in weight, slipped a halter over the poor beast's head.

"I could get a strap around him!" Harry suggested, moving out cautiously on the plank.

"All right, my lad, go ahead," Peter told him, passing the big strap over to Bert, who in turn passed it on to Harry.

It was no easy matter to get the strap in place, but with much tugging and splashing of mud Harry succeeded. Then the ropes were attached and everybody pulled vigorously.

"Get up, Ginger! Get up, Ginger!" Peter called lustily, but Ginger only seemed to flop in deeper, through his efforts to raise himself.

"Guess we'll have to get Billy to pull," Uncle Daniel suggested, and Mr. Bobbsey hurried back to the road to unhitch the other horse.

"Don't let Billy fall in!" exclaimed Nan, who was much excited over the accident.

"Can't I go, papa?" Freddie pleaded. "I'll stay away from the edge!"

"You better stay in the wagon; the horse might cut up when he gets out," the father warned Freddie, who reluctantly gave in.

Soon Billy was hitched to the ropes, and with a few kind words from Uncle Daniel the big white horse strained forward, pulling Ginger to his feet as he did so.

"Hurrah!" shouted Freddie from the wagon. "Billy is a circus horse, isn't he, Uncle Dan?"

"He's a good boy," the uncle called back patting Billy affectionately, while Mr. Bobbsey and the boys loosened the straps. The other horse lay on the blankets, and Peter rubbed him with all his might, to save a chill as he told the boys.

Then, after receiving many thanks for the help given, the Bobbseys once more started off toward the farm.

"Hot work," Uncle Daniel remarked to the ladies, as he mopped his forehead.

"I'm so glad you could help Peter," Aunt Sarah told him, "for he does seem to have so much trouble."

"All kinds of things happen in the country," Harry remarked, as Billy headed off for home.

At each house along the way boys would call out to Harry, asking him about going fishing, or berrying, or some other sport, so that Bert felt a good time was in store for him, as the boys were about his own age and seemed so agreeable.

"Nice fellows," Harry remarked by way of introducing Bert.

"They seem so," Bert replied, cordially.

"We've made up a lot of sports," Harry went on, "and we were only waiting for you to come to start out. We've planned a picnic for tomorrow."

"Here we are," called Uncle Daniel as Billy turned into the pretty driveway in front of the Bobbseys' country home. On each side of the drive grew straight lines of boxwood, and back of this hedge were beautiful flowers, shining out grandly now in the July sun.

"Hello, Martha!" called the visitors, as the faithful old servant appeared on the broad white veranda.

"Got here at last!" she exclaimed, taking

Dinah's lunch basket.

"Glad to see you, Martha," Dinah told her. "You see, I had to come along. And Snoop too, our kitty."

"The more the merrier," replied the other, "and there's lots of room for all."

"Starved to death!" Harry laughed, as the odor of a fine dinner reached him.

"We'll wash up a bit and join you in a few minutes, ladies," Uncle Daniel said, in his polite way. The horse accident had given plenty of need for a washing up.

"Got Snoop this time," Freddie lisped, knocking the cover off the box and petting the frightened little black cat. "Hungry, Snoopy?" he asked, pressing his baby cheek to the soft fur.

"Bring the poor kitty out to the kitchen," Martha told him. "I'll get him a nice saucer of fresh milk." And so it happened, as usual, Snoop had his meal first, just as he had had on the Pullman car. Soon after this Martha went outside and rang a big dinner bell that all the men and boys could hear. And then the first vacation dinner was served in the long old-fashioned dining room.

CHAPTER 6

FRISKY

ALTHOUGH they were tired from their journey, the children had no idea of resting on that beautiful afternoon, so promptly after dinner the baggage was opened, and vacation clothes were put on. Bert, of course, was ready first, and soon he and Harry were running down the road to meet the other boys and perfect their plans for the picnic.

Nan began her pleasures by exploring the flower gardens with Uncle Daniel.

"I pride myself on those zinnias," the uncle told Nan. "Just see those yellows, and those pinks. Some are as big as dahlias, aren't they?"

"They are just beautiful, uncle," Nan replied, in real admiration. "I have always loved zinnias. And they last so long?"

"All summer. Then, what do you think of my sweet peas?"

So they went from one flower bed to another, and Nan thought she had never before seen so

31

many pretty plants together.

Flossie and Freddie were out in the barnyard with Aunt Sarah.

"Oh, auntie, what queer little chickens!" Flossie exclaimed, pouting to a lot of pigeons that were eagerly eating corn with the chickens.

"Those are Harry's homer pigeons," the aunt explained. "Some day we must go off to the woods and let the birds fly home with a letter to Dinah and Martha."

"Oh, please do it now," Freddie urged, always in a hurry for things.

"We couldn't today, dear," Aunt Sarah told him. "Come, let me show you our new little calf."

"Let me ride her?" Freddie asked, as they reached the animal.

"Calfs aren't for riding, they're for milk," Flossie spoke up.

"Yes, this one drinks plenty of milk," Aunt Sarah said, while Frisky, the calf, rubbed her head kindly against Aunt Sarah's skirts.

"Then let me take her for a walk," Freddie pleaded, much in love with the pretty creature.

"And they don't walk either," Flossie persisted. "They mostly run."

"I could just hold the rope, couldn't I, Aunt Sarah?"

"If you keep away from the barnyard gate, and

hold her very tight," was the consent given finally, much to Freddie's delight.

"Nice Frisky," he told the calf, petting her fondly. "Pretty calf, will you let Snoop play with you?" Frisky was sniffing suspiciously all the time, and Aunt Sarah had taken Flossie in the barn to see the chickens' nests.

"Come, Frisky, take a walk," suggested Freddie, and quite obediently the little cow walked along. But suddenly Frisky spied the open gate and the lovely green grass outside.

Without a moment's warning the calf threw her hind legs up in the air, then bolted straight for the gate, dragging Freddie along after her.

"Whoa, Frisky! Whoa!" yelled Freddie, but the calf ran right along.

"Hold tight, Freddie!" called Flossie, as she and Aunt Sarah appeared on the scene.

"Whoa, whoa!" yelled the little boy constantly, but he might as well have called "Get app," for Frisky was going so fast now that poor little Freddie's hands were all but bleeding from the rough rope.

"Look out, Freddie! Let go!" called Aunt Sarah as she saw Frisky heading for the apple tree.

The next minute Frisky made a dash around the tree, once, then again, winding the rope as she went, and throwing Freddie out with force against the side of the terrace.

"Oh," Freddie moaned feebly.

"Are you dead?" cried Flossie, running up with tears in his eyes.

"Oh," moaned the boy again, turning over with much trouble as Aunt Sarah lifted him.

"Oh," he murmured once more, "oh—catch—Frisky!"

"Never mind her," Aunt Sarah said, anxiously. "Are you hurt, dear?"

"No—not—a bit. But look! There goes Frisky! Catch her!"

"Your poor little hands!" Flossie almost cried, kissing the red blisters. "See, they're cut!"

"Firemen have to slide on ropes!" Freddie spoke up, recovering himself, "and I'm going to be a fireman. I was one that time, because I tried to save somebody and didn't care if I got hurted!"

"You are a brave little boy," Aunt Sarah assured him. "You just sit here with sister while I try to get that naughty Frisky before she spoils the garden."

By this time the calf was almost lost to them, as she plunged in and out of the pretty hedges. Fortunately Bert and Harry just turned in the gate.

"Runaway calf! Runaway calf!" called the boys. "Stop the runaway!" and instantly a half dozen other boys appeared, and all started in pursuit.

But Frisky knew how to run, besides she had

the advantage of a good start, and now she just dashed along as if the affair was the biggest joke of her life.

"The river! The river!" called the boys. "She'll jump in!" and indeed the pretty Meadow Brook, or river, that ran along some feet lower than the Bobbseys' house, on the other side of the highway, was now dangerously near the runaway calf.

There was a heavy thicket a few feet further up, and as the boys squeezed in and out of the bushes Frisky plunged into this piece of wood.

"Oh, she's gone now, sure!" called Harry. "Listen!"

Sure enough there was a splash!

Frisky must be in the river!

It took some time to reach the spot where the fall might have sounded from, and the boys made their way heavy-hearted, for all loved the pretty little Frisky.

"There's footprints!" Bert discovered, emerging from the thick bush.

"And they end here!" Harry finished, indicating the very brink of the river.

"She's gone!"

"But how could she drown so quickly?" Bert asked.

"Guess that's the channel," Tom Mason, one of the neighbors' boys, answered.

"Listen! Thought I heard something in the bushes!" Bert whispered.

But no welcome sound came to tell that poor Frisky was hiding in the brushwood. With heavy hearts the boys turned away. They didn't even feel like talking, somehow. They had counted on bringing the calf back in triumph.

When Flossie and Freddie saw them come back without Frisky they just had to cry and no one could stop them.

"I tried to be a fireman!" blubbered Freddie. "I didn't care if the rope hurted my hands either!"

"If only I didn't go in to see the chickens' nests," Flossie whimpered, "I could have helped Freddie!"

"Never you mind, little ones," Dinah told them. "I'll go and fetch that Frisky back tomorrow. You just don't cry any more, but eat your supper and take a good sleep, 'cause we're going to have a picnic tomorrow you know, don't you?"

The others tried to comfort the little ones too, and Uncle Daniel said he knew where he could buy another calf just like Frisky, so after a little while Freddie felt better and even laughed when Martha made the white cat Fluffy and Snoop play ball in the big long kitchen.

"I'm goin' to pray Frisky will come back," Nan told her little brother when she kissed him goodnight, "and maybe the dear Lord will find her for you."

"Oh, yes, Nannie, do ask Him," pleaded Freddie, "and tell Him—tell Him if He'll do it this time, I'll be so good I won't never need to bother Him anymore."

Freddie meant very well, but it sounded strange, and made Aunt Sarah say, "The Lord bless the little darling!" Then night came and an eventful day closed in on our dear little Bobbseys.

"Seems as if something else ought to happen tonight," Bert remarked to Harry as they prepared to retire. "This was such a full day, wasn't it?"

"It's early yet," Harry answered, "and it's never late here until it's time to get early again."

"Sounds so strange to hear—those—those—"

"Crickets," Harry told him, "and tree toads and katydids. Oh, there's lots to listen to if you shouldn't feel sleepy."

The house was now all quiet, and even the boys had ceased whispering. Suddenly there was a noise in the driveway!

The next minute someone called out in the night!

"Hello there! All asleep! Wake up, somebody!"

Even Freddie did wake up and ran into his mother's room.

"Come down here, Mr. Bobbsey," the voice continued.

"Oh, is that you, Peter? I'll be down directly," called back Uncle Daniel, who very soon after appeared on the front porch.

"Well, I declare!" Uncle Daniel exclaimed, loud enough for all the listeners at the window to hear. "So you've got her? Well, I'm very glad indeed. Especially on the boys' account."

"Yes," spoke out Peter Burns, "I went in the barn a while ago with the lantern, and if there wasn't your calf asleep with mine as cozy as could be. I brought her over tonight for fear you might miss her and get to lookin', otherwise I wouldn't have disturbed you."

By this time the man from the barn was up and out too, and he took Frisky back to her own bed, but not until the little calf had been taken far out on the front lawn so that Freddie could see her from the window "to make sure."

"The Lord did bring her back," Freddie told his mamma as she kissed him goodnight again and put him in his bed, happier this time than before. "And I promised to be awful good to pay Him for His trouble," the sleepy boy murmured.

Flossie had been asleep about two hours when she suddenly called to her mother.

"What is it, my dear?" asked Mrs. Bobbsey.

"Somebody is playing the piano," answered the little girl. "Who is it?"

"Nobody is playing. You must be dreaming," answered the mother, and smiled to herself.

"No, I am sure I heard the piano," insisted Flossie.

Mother and daughter listened, but could hear nothing.

"You were surely dreaming," said Mrs. Bobbsey. "Come, I will tuck you in again," and she did so.

But was Flossie dreaming? Let us wait and see.

CHAPTER 7

A COUNTRY PICNIC

WHEN morning came everyone was astir early, for not only was a happy day promised, but there was Frisky, the runaway, to be looked over. Mr. Richard Bobbsey, Freddie's father, left on an early train for Lakeport, and would not come back to Meadow Brook until Saturday afternoon.

"Let me go out and see Frisky," Freddie insisted, even before his breakfast had been served. "I want to be sure it's her."

"Yes, that's her," Freddie admitted, "'cause there's the rope that cut my hands when I was a real fireman!"

Frisky didn't seem to care a bit about ropes or firemen, but just chewed and chewed like all cows do, as if there was nothing in this world to do but eat.

"Come on, sonny," called Dinah. "You can help me pick the radishes for breakfast," and presently our little boy, with the kind-hearted

41

maid, was up in the garden looking for the best radishes of the early crop.

"See, Freddie," said Dinah. "The red ones show above the ground. And we must only pull the ones with the big leaves, 'cause they're ripe."

Freddie bent down so close to find the radishes that a disturbed toad hopped right up at his nose.

"Oh!" he cried, frightened. "Dinah, was that—a—a—a snake?"

"Snake, child! That was a poor little toad—more scared than you are," and she pointed to the big dock leaf under which the hop-toad was now hiding.

"Let's pick beans," Freddie suggested, liking the garden work.

"Not beans for breakfast," laughed Dinah.

"That stuff there, then," the boy persisted, pointing to the soft green leaves of early lettuce.

"Well, I don't know. Martha didn't say so, but it sure does look pretty. Yes, I guess we can pick some for salad," and so Dinah showed Freddie how to cut the lettuce heads off and leave the stalks to grow again.

"Out early," laughed Uncle Daniel, seeing the youngest member of the family coming down the garden path with the small basket of vegetables.

"Is it?" Freddie asked, meaning early of

course, in his queer way of saying things without words.

"See! See!" called Nan and Flossie, running down the cross path back of the cornfield. "Such big ones!" Nan exclaimed, referring to the luscious red strawberries in the white dish she held.

"Look at mine," insisted Flossie. "Aren't they bigger?"

"Fine!" ejaculated Dinah.

"But my redishes are—are—redder," argued Freddie, who was not to be outdone by his sisters.

"Ours are sweeter," laughed Nan, trying to tease her little brother.

"Ours are—ours are—"

"Hotter," put in Dinah, which ended the argument.

Bert and Harry had also been out gathering for breakfast, and returned now with a basket of lovely fresh watercress.

"We can't eat 'em all," Martha told the boys. "But they'll go good in the picnic lunch."

What a pretty breakfast table it was! Such berries, such lettuce, such watercress, and the radishes!

"Too bad papa had to go so early," Bert remarked. "He just loves green stuff."

"So does Frisky," put in Freddie, and he wondered why everyone laughed.

After breakfast the lunch baskets were put up, and while Bert and Harry, Nan and Aunt Sarah, went to invite the neighboring children, Flossie and Freddie were just busy jumping around the kitchen, where Dinah and Martha were making them laugh merrily with funny little stories.

Snoop and Fluffy had become good friends, and now lay close together on the kitchen hearth. Dinah said they were just like two babies, only not so much trouble.

"Put peaches in my basket, Dinah," Freddie ordered.

"And strawberries in mine," added Flossie.

"Now, you young ones just wait!" Dinah told them. "And when you get out in the woods if you haven't enough to eat you can just climb a tree and cut down—"

"Wood!" put in Freddie innocently, while Martha said that was about all that could be found in the woods in July.

The boys had come in from inviting the "other fellers," when Uncle Daniel proposed a feature for the picnic.

"How would you like to take two homer pigeons along?" he asked them. "You can send a note back to Martha to say what time you will be home."

"Jolly!" chorused the boys, all instantly making

a run for the pigeon house.

"Wait!" Harry told the visitors. "We must be careful not to scare them." Then he went inside the wire cage with a handful of corn.

"See—de—con, see—de—con!" called the boys softly, imitating the queer sounds made by the doves cooing.

Harry tossed the corn inside the cage, and as the light and dark homers he wanted tasted the food Harry lowered the little door, and took the birds safely in his arms.

"Now, Bert, you can get the quills," he told his cousin. "Go into the chicken yard and look for two long goose feathers. Tom Mason, you can go in the kitchen and ask Dinah for a piece of tissue paper and a spool of silk thread."

Each boy started off to fulfill his commission, not knowing exactly what for until all came together in the barnyard again.

"Now, Bert," went on Harry, "write very carefully on the slip of paper the message for Martha. Have you a soft pencil?"

Bert found that he had one, and so following his cousin's dictation he wrote on one slip: "Have dinner ready at five." And on the other he wrote: "John, come for us at four."

"Now," continued Harry, "roll the slips up fine enough to go in the goose quills."

This was done with much difficulty, as the quills were very narrow, but the task was finally finished.

"All ready now," concluded Harry, "to put the letters in the box," and very gently he tied with the silken thread one quill under the wing of each pigeon. Only one feather was used to tie the thread to, and the light quill, the thin paper, and the soft silk made a parcel so very small and light in weight that the pigeons were no way inconvenienced by the messages.

"Now we'll put them in this basket, and they're ready for the picnic," Harry announced to his much interested companions. Then all started for the house with Harry and the basket in the lead.

John, the stableman, was at the door now with the big hay wagon, which had been chosen as the best thing to take the jolly party in. There was nice fresh hay in the bottom, and seats at the side for the grown folks, while the little ones nestled in the sweet-smelling hay like live birds.

"It's like a kindergarten party," laughed Nan, as the "birds' nests" reminded her of one of the mother plays.

"No, 'tain't!" Freddie corrected, for he really was not fond of the kindergarten. "It's just like a picnic," he finished.

Besides the Bobbseys there were Tom Mason,

Jack Hopkins, and August Stout, friends of Harry. Then, there were Mildred Manners and Mabel Herold, who went as Nan's guests; little Roy Mason was Freddie's company, and Bessie Dimple went with Flossie. The little pigeons kept cooing every now and then, but made no attempt to escape from Harry's basket.

It was a beautiful day, and the long ride through the country was indeed a merry one. Along the way people called out pleasantly from farmhouses, for everybody in Meadow Brook knew the Bobbseys.

"That's their cousins from the city," little boys and girls along the way would say.

"Haven't they pretty clothes!" the girls were sure to add.

"Let's stop for a drink at the spring," suggested August Stout, who was stout by name and nature, and always loved a good drink of water.

The children tumbled out of the wagon safely, and were soon waiting turns at the spring.

There was a round basin built of stones and quite deep. Into this the clear sprinkling water dropped from a little cave in the hill above. On top of the cave a large flat stone was placed. This kept the little waterfall clean and free from the falling leaves.

"Oh, what a cute little pond!" Freddie

exclaimed, for he had never seen a real spring before.

"That's a spring," Flossie informed him, although that was all she knew about it.

The big boys were not long dipping their faces in and getting a drink of the cool, clear water, but the girls had to take their hats off, roll up their sleeves, and go through a "regular performance," as Harry said, before they could make up their minds to dip into the water. Mabel brought up her supply with her hands, but when Nan tried it her hands leaked, and the result was her fresh white frock got wet. Flossie's curls tumbled in both sides, and when she had finished she looked as if she had taken a plunge at the seashore.

"Let me! Let me!" cried Freddie impatiently, and without further warning he thrust his yellow head in the spring clear up to his neck!

"Oh, Freddie!" yelled Nan, grabbing him by the heels and thus saving a more serious accident.

"Oh! Oh! Oh!" spluttered Freddie, nearly choked, "I'm drowned!" and the water seemed to be running out of his eyes, nose, and ears all at once.

"Oh, Freddie!" was all Mrs. Bobbsey could say, as a shower of clean handkerchiefs was sent from the hay wagon to dry the "drowned" boy.

"Just like the flour barrel!" laughed Bert,

referring to the funny accident that befell Freddie the winter before, as told in my other book "The Bobbsey Twins."

"Only that was a dry bath and this a wet one," Nan remarked, as Freddie's curls were shook out in the sun.

"Did you get a drink?" asked August, whose invitation to drink had caused the mishap.

"Yep!" answered Freddie bravely, "and I was a real fireman, too, that time, 'cause they always get soaked. Don't they, Bert?"

Being assured they did, the party once more started off for the woods. It was getting to be all woods now, only a driveway breaking through the pines, maples, and chestnut trees that abounded in that section.

"Just turn in there, John!" Harry directed, as a particularly thick group of trees appeared. Here were chosen the picnic grounds and all the things taken from the wagon, and before John was out of sight on the return home the children had established their camp and were flying about the woods like little fairies.

"Let's build a furnace," Jack Hopkins suggested.

"Let's," said all the boys, who immediately set out carrying stones and piling them up to build the stove. There were plenty of woods about, and when the fire was built, the raw potatoes that Harry had secretly brought along were roasted, finer than any oven could cook them.

Mrs. Bobbsey and Aunt Sarah had spread the tablecloth on the grass, and were now busy opening the baskets and arranging the places. There were so many pretty little nooks to explore in the woods that Mrs. Bobbsey had to warn the children not to get too far away.

"Are there giants?" Freddie asked.

"No, but there are very dark lonely places in the woods and little boys might find snakes."

"And bears!" put in Freddie, to which remark his mother said, "Perhaps," because there really might be bears in a woods so close to the mountains.

CHAPTER 8

FUN IN THE WOODS

"DINNER served in the dining car!" called Bert through the woods, imitating the call of the porter on the Pullman car.

"All ready!" echoed the other boys, banging on an old boiler like the Turks do, instead of ringing a bell.

"Oh, how pretty!" the girls all exclaimed, as they beheld the "feast in the forest," as Nan put it. And indeed it was pretty, for at each place was set a long plume of fern leaves with wood violets at the end, and what could be more beautiful than such a decoration?

"Potatoes first!" Harry announced. "Because they may get cold," and at this order everybody broke the freshly roasted potatoes into the paper napkins and touched it up with the extra butter that had come along.

"Simply fine!" declared Nan, with the air of one who knew. Now, my old readers will remember how Nan baked such good cake. So she ought to be an authority on baked potatoes, don't you think?

Next came the sandwiches, with the watercress Harry and Bert had gathered before breakfast, then (and this was a surprise) hot chocolate! This was brought out in Martha's cider jug, and heated in a kettle over the boys' stone furnace.

"It must be fun to camp out," Mabel Herold remarked.

"Yes, just think of the dishes saved," added Mildred Manners, who always had so many dishes to do at home.

"And we really don't need them," Nan argued, passing her tin cup on to Flossie.

"Think how the soldiers get along!" Bert put in.

"And the firemen!" lisped Freddie, who never forgot the heroes of flame and water.

Of course everybody was either sitting on the grass or on a "soft stump." These latter conveniences had been brought by the boys for Aunt Sarah and Mrs. Bobbsey.

"What's that!" exclaimed little Flossie, as something was plainly moving under the table-cloth.

"A snake, a snake!" called everybody at once, for indeed under the white linen was plainly to be seen the creeping form of a reptile. While the girls made a run for safety the boys carefully lifted the cloth and went for his snakeship.

"There he is! There he is!" shouted Tom Mason, as the thing tried to crawl under the stump lately used as a seat by Mrs. Bobbsey.

"Whack him!" called August Stout, who, armed with a good club, made straight for the stump.

"Look out! He's a big fellow!" Harry declared, as the snake attempted to get upright.

The boys fell back a little now, and as the snake actually stood on the tip of his tail, as they do before striking, Harry sprang forward and dealt him a heavy blow right on the head that laid the intruder flat.

"At him, boys! At him!" called Jack Hopkins, while the snake lay wriggling in the grass, and the boys, making good use of the stunning blow Harry had dealt, piled on as many more blows as their clubs could wield.

All this time the girls and ladies were over on a knoll "high and dry," as Nan said, and now, when assured that the snake was done for, they could hardly be induced to come and look at him.

"He's a beauty!" Harry declared, as the boys actually stretched the creature out to measure him. Bert had a rule, and when the snake was measured up he was found to be five feet long!

"He's a black racer!" Jack Hopkins announced, and the others said they guessed he was.

"Lucky we saw him first!" remarked Harry. "Racers are very poisonous!"

"Let's go home. There might be more!" pleaded Flossie, but the boys said the snake hunt was the best fun at the picnic.

"Goodness!" exclaimed Harry suddenly, "we forgot to let the pigeons loose!" and so saying he ran for the basket of birds that hung on the low limb of a pretty maple. First Harry made sure the messages were safe under each bird's wing, then he called:

"All ready!"

Snap! went something that sounded like a shot (but it wasn't), and then away flew the pretty birds to take the messages home to John and Martha. The shot was only a dry stick that Tom Mason snapped to imitate a gun, as they do at bicycle races, but the effect was quite startling and made the girls jump.

"It won't take long for them to get home!" said Bert, watching the birds fly away.

"They'll get lost!" cried Freddie.

"No, they won't. They know which way we came," Nan explained.

"But they was shut up in the basket," argued Freddie.

"Yet they could see," Nan told him.

"Can pigeons see when they're asleep?" inquired the little fellow.

"Maybe," Nan answered.

"Then I'd like to have pigeon eyes," he finished, thinking to himself how fine it would be to see everything going on around and be fast asleep too.

"Oh, mamma, come quick!" called Flossie, running along a path at the edge of the wood. "There's a tree over there pouring water, and it isn't raining a drop!"

Everybody set out now to look at the wonderful tree, which was soon discovered where Flossie had found it.

"There it is!" she exclaimed. "See the water dropping down!"

"A maple tree," Harry informed them, "and that sap is what they make maple sugar out of."

"Oh, catch it!" called Freddie, promptly holding his cap under the drops.

"It would take a good deal to make a sugar cake," Harry said, "but maybe we can get enough of it to make a little cake for Freddie."

At this the country boys began looking around for young maples, and as small limbs of the trees were broken the girls caught the drops in their tin cups. It took quite a while to get a little, but by putting it all together a cupful was finally gathered.

"Now we will put it in a clean milk bottle," Mrs. Bobbsey said, "and maybe we can make a maple syrup cake tomorrow."

"Let's have a game of hide-and-seek," Nan suggested.

In a twinkling every boy and girl was hidden behind a tree, and Nan found herself "It." Of course it took a big tree to hide the girls' dresses, and Nan had no trouble in spying Mildred first. Soon the game was going along merrily, and the boys and girls were out of breath trying to get "home free."

"Where's Roy?" exclaimed Tom Mason, the little boy's brother.

"Hiding somewhere," Bessie ventured, for it only seemed a minute before when the little fat boy who was Freddie's companion had been with the others.

"But where he is?" they all soon exclaimed in alarm, as call after call brought no answer.

"Over at the maple tree!" Harry thought.

"Down at the spring," Nan said.

"Looking for flowers," Flossie guessed.

But all these spots were searched, and the little boy was not found.

"Oh, maybe the giants have stoled him!" Freddie cried.

"Or maybe the children's hawk has took him away," Flossie sobbed.

Meanwhile everybody searched and searched, but no Roy could they find.

"The boat!" suddenly exclaimed Tom, making a dash for the pond that ran along at the foot of a steep hill.

"There he is! There he is!" the brother yelled, as getting over the edge of the hill Tom was now in full view of the pond.

"And in the boat," called Harry, close at Tom's heels.

"He's drifting away!" screamed Bert. "Oh, quick, save him!"

Just as the boys said, the little fellow was in the boat and drifting.

He did not seem to realize his danger, for as he floated along he ran his little fat hand through the water as happily as if he had been in a steam launch, talking to the captain.

"Can you swim?" the boys asked Bert, who of course had learned that useful art long ago.

"He's quite a long way out," Tom said. "But we must be careful not to frighten him. See, he has left the oars here. Bert and I can carry one out and swim with one hand. Harry and Jack, can you manage the other?"

The boys said they could, and quickly as the

heaviest clothes could be thrown off they were striking out in the little lake toward the baby in the boat. He was only Freddie's age, you know, and perhaps more of a baby than the good-natured Bobbsey boy.

"Sit still, Roy," called the anxious girl from the shore, fearing Roy would upset the boat as the boys neared him. It was hard work to swim and carry oars, but our brave boys managed to do it in time to save Roy. For not a great way down the stream were an old water wheel and a dam. Should the boat drift there what would become of little Roy?

Mrs. Bobbsey and Aunt Sarah were worrying over this as the boys were making their way to the boat.

"Easy now!" called Bert. "Here we are," and at that moment the first pair of swimmers climbed carefully into the boat, one from each side, so as not to tip it over. Jack and Harry were not long in following, and as the boys all sat in the pretty green rowboat with their white underclothing answering for athletic suits, they looked just like a crew of real oarsmen.

"Hurrah, hurrah!" came shout after shout from the bank. Then as the girls heard the rumble of wheels through the grove they all hurried off to gather up the stuff quickly, and be ready to start as soon as the boys dressed again. The wet underclothing, of course, was carried home in one of the empty baskets that Freddie ran back over the hill with to save the tired boys the extra walk.

"Here they are! Here they are!" called the girls as the two little fellows, Roy and Freddie, with the basket of wet clothes between them, marched first; then came the two pairs of athletes who proved they were good swimmers by pushing the heavy oars safely to the drifting boat.

"And all the things that happened!" exclaimed Flossie, as John handed her into the hay wagon.

"That made the picnic lively!" declared John, "and all's well that ends well, you know." So the picnic was over, and all were happy and tired enough to go to bed early that night, as Nan said, seeing the little ones falling asleep in the hay wagon on their way home.

CHAPTER 9

FOURTH OF JULY

THE day following the picnic was July third, and as the Meadow Brook children were pretty well tired out from romping in the woods, they were glad of a day's rest before entering upon the festivities of Independence Day.

"How much have you got?" Tom Mason asked the Bobbsey boys.

"Fifty cents together, twenty-five cents each," Harry announced.

"Well, I've got thirty-five, and we had better get our stuff early, for Stimpson sold out before noon last year," concluded Tom.

"I have to get torpedoes for Freddie and Flossie, and Chinese firecrackers for Nan," Bert remarked, as they started for the little country grocery store.

"I guess I'll buy a few snakes, they look so funny coiling out," Tom said.

"I'm going to have skyrockets and Roman candles. Everybody said they were the prettiest last year," said Harry.

"If they have red fire I must get some of it for the girls," thoughtful Bert remarked.

But at the store the boys had to take just what they could get, as Stimpson's supply was very limited.

"Let's make up a parade!" someone suggested, and this being agreed upon the boys started a canvass from house to house, to get all the boys along Meadow Brook Road to take part in the procession.

"Can the little ones come too?" August Stout asked, because he always had to look out for his small brother when there was any danger like fireworks around.

"Yes, and we're goin' to let the girls march in a division by themselves," Bert told him. "My sister Nan is going to be captain, and we'll leave all the girls' parts to her."

"Be sure and bring your flag," Harry cautioned Jack Hopkins.

"How would the goat wagons do?" Jack asked.

"Fine. We could let Roy and Freddie ride in them," said Bert. "Tell any of the other fellows who have goat teams to bring them along too."

"Eight o'clock sharp at our lane," Harry told them for the place and time of meeting. Then they went along to finish the arrangements.

"Don't tell the boys," Nan whispered to Mildred, as they too made their way to Stimpson's.

"Won't they be surprised?" exclaimed Mabel.

"Yes, and I am going to carry a real Betsy Ross flag, one with thirteen stars, you know."

"Oh, yes, Betsy Ross made the first flag, didn't she?" remarked Mildred, trying to catch up on history.

"We'll have ten big girls," Nan counted. "Then with Flossie as Liberty we will want Bessie and Nettie for her assistants."

"Attendants," Mabel corrected, for she had seen a city parade like that once.

It was a busy day for everybody, and when Mr. Bobbsey came up on the train from Lakeport that evening he carried boxes and boxes of fireworks for the boys and girls, and even some for the grown folks too.

The girls could hardly sleep that night, they were so excited over their part, but the boys of course were used to that sort of thing, and only slept sounder with the fun in prospect.

"Are you awake, Bert?" called Harry, so early the next morning that the sun was hardly up yet.

"Yep," replied the cousin, jumping out of bed and hastily dressing for the firing of the first gun.

The boys crept through the house very quietly,

then ran to the barn for their ammunition. Three big giant firecrackers were placed in the road directly in front of the house.

"Be careful!" whispered Bert. "They're full of powder."

But Harry was always careful with fireworks, and when he touched the fuses to the "cannons" he made away quickly before they exploded.

Bang! Bang! Bang!

"Hurrah!" shouted Freddie, answering the call from his window. "I'll be right down!"

All the others too were aroused by the first "guns," so that in a very short time there were many boys in the road, firing so many kinds of firecrackers that Meadow Brook resounded like a real war fort under fire.

"Ouch!" yelled Tom Mason, the first one to burn his fingers. "A sisser caught me right on the thumb."

But such small accidents were not given much attention, and soon Tom was lighting the little red crackers as merrily as before.

"Go on back, girls!" called Bert. "You'll get your dresses burnt if you don't."

The girls were coming too near the battlements then, and Bert did well to warn them off.

Freddie and Flossie were having a great time throwing their little torpedoes at Mr. Bobbsey and

Uncle Daniel, who were seated on the piazza watching the sport. Snoop and Fluffy too came in for a scare, for Freddie tossed a couple of torpedoes on the kitchen hearth where the kittens were sleeping.

The boys were having such fun they could hardly be induced to come in for breakfast, but they finally did stop long enough to eat a spare meal.

"It's time to get ready!" whispered Nan to Bert, for the parade had been kept secret from the grown folks.

At the girls' place of meeting, the coach house, Nan found all her company waiting and anxious to dress.

"Just tie your scarves loose under your left arm," ordered Captain Nan, and the girls quickly obeyed like true cadets. The broad red-white-and-blue bunting was very pretty over the girls' white dresses, and indeed the "cadets" looked as if they would outdo the "regulars" unless the boys too had surprises in store.

"Where's Nettie?" suddenly asked Nan, missing a poor little girl who had been invited.

"She wouldn't come because she had no white dress," Mildred answered.

"Oh, what a shame; she'll be so disappointed! Besides, we need her to make a full line," Nan said. "Just wait a minute. Lock the door after me," and before the others knew what she was going to do, Nan ran off to the house, got one of her own white dresses, rolled it up neatly, and was over the fields to Nettie's house in a few minutes. When Nan came back she brought Nettie with her, and not one of her companions knew it was Nan's dress that Nettie wore.

Soon all the scarves were tied and the flags arranged. Then Flossie had to be dressed.

She wore a light blue dress with gold stars on it, and on her pretty yellow curls she had a real Liberty crown. Then she had the cleanest, brightest flag, and what a pretty picture she made!

"Oh, isn't she sweet!" all the girls exclaimed in admiration, and indeed she was a little beauty in her Liberty costume.

"There go the drums!" Nan declared. "We must be careful to get down the lane without being seen." This was easily managed, and now the girls and boys met at the end of the lane.

"Hurrah! Hurrah!" shouted the boys, beating the drums and blowing their horns to welcome the girls.

"Oh, don't you look fine!" exclaimed Harry, who was captain of the boys.

"And don't you too!" Nan answered, for indeed the boys had such funny big hats on and so many flags and other red-white-and-blue things, that they too made a fine appearance.

"And Freddie!" exclaimed the girls. "Isn't he a lovely Uncle Sam!"

Freddie was dressed in the striped suit Uncle Sam always wears, and had on his yellow curls a tall white hat. He was to ride in Jack Hopkins' goat wagon.

"Fall in!" called Harry, and at the word all the companies fell in line.

"Cadets first," ordered the captain.

Then Flossie walked the very first one. After her came Nan and her company. (No one noticed that Nettie's eyes were a little red from crying. She had been so disappointed at first when she thought she couldn't go in the parade.) After the girls came Freddie as Uncle Sam, in the goat wagon led by Bert (for fear the goat might run away), then fifteen boys, all with drums or fifes or some other things with which to make a noise. Roy was in the second division with his wagon, and last of all came the funniest thing.

A boy dressed up like a bear with a big sign on him:

TEDDY!

He had a gun under his arm and looked too comical for anything.

It was quite warm to wear a big fur robe and false face, but under this was Jack Hopkins, the bear Teddy, and he didn't mind being warm when he made everybody laugh so.

"Right foot, left foot, right foot, forward march!" called Nan, and the procession started up the path straight for the Bobbsey house.

"Goodness gracious! Do come see the children! Ha, ha! That sure is a parade!" called Dinah, running through the house to the front door to view the procession.

"Oh, isn't it just beautiful!" Martha echoed close at Dinah's heels.

"My!" exclaimed Mrs. Bobbsey. "How did they ever get made up so pretty!"

"And look at Flossie!" exclaimed Aunt Sarah.

"And see Freddie!" put in Uncle Daniel.

"Oh, we must get the camera!" Mr. Bobbsey declared, while the whole household, all excited, stood out on the porch when the parade advanced.

Such drumming and such tooting of fifes and horns!

Freddie's chariot was now in line with the front stoop, and he raised his tall hat to the ladies like a real Uncle Sam.

"Oh, the bear! The bear!" called everybody, as they saw "Teddy" coming up.

"That's great," continued Uncle Daniel.

By this time Mr. Bobbsey had returned with the camera.

"Halt!" called Harry, and the procession stood still.

"Look this way. There now, all ready," said Mr. Bobbsey, and snap went the camera on as pretty a picture as ever covered a plate.

"Right wheel! Forward march!" called Nan again, and amid drumming and tooting the procession started off to parade through the center of Meadow Brook.

CHAPTER 10

A GREAT DAY

NEVER before had such a parade been seen in the little country place, and all along the road cheer after cheer greeted our young friends, for even the few old soldiers who lived in Meadow Brook enjoyed the children's Fourth of July fun.

By lunchtime the procession had covered all the ground planned, so from the post office the cadets and regulars started back over the shady country road.

And at home they found a surprise awaiting them!

Ice cream on the lawn for everybody in the parade.

Aunt Sarah and Uncle Daniel had set out all the garden benches, and with the two kinds of ice cream made by Dinah and Martha, besides the cookies and jumbles Aunt Sarah supplied, with ice-cold lemonade that John passed around, surely the tired little soldiers and cadets had splendid refreshment!

"My goat almost runned away!" lisped Freddie. "But I held on tight like a real fireman."

"And mine wanted to stop and eat grass in the middle of the big parade," Roy told them.

"Now eat up your ice cream. Nettie, have some more? Jack, you surely need two plates after carrying that bearskin," said Uncle Daniel.

The youngsters did not have to be urged to eat some more of the good things, and so it took quite a while to "finish up the rations," as Uncle Daniel said.

"They're goin' to shoot the old cannon off, father," Harry told Uncle Daniel, "and we're all going over on the pond bank to see them, at three o'clock."

"They're foolish to put powder in that old cracked gun," remarked Uncle Daniel. "Take care, if you go over, that you all keep at a safe distance."

It was not long until three o'clock, and then when all the red-white-and-blue things had been stored away for another year, the boys hurried off to see Peter Burns fire the old cannon.

Quite a crowd of people had gathered about the pond bank, which was a high green wall like that which surrounds a reservoir.

Peter was busy stuffing the powder in the old gun, and all the others looked on anxiously.

"Let's go up in that big limb of the willow

tree," suggested Bert. "We can see it all then, and be out of range of the fire."

So the boys climbed up in the low willow that leaned over the pond bank.

"They're almost ready," Harry said, seeing the crowd scatter.

"Look out!" yelled Peter, getting hold of the long string that would fire the gun.

Peter gave it a tug, then another.

Everybody held their breath, expecting to hear an awful bang, but the gun didn't go off.

Very cautiously Peter stepped nearer the cannon to see what might be the matter, when the next instant with a terrific report the whole cannon flew up in the air!

Peter fell back! His hat seemed to go up with the gun!

"Oh, he's killed!" yelled the people.

"Poor Peter!" gasped Harry.

"He ought to know better!" said Mr. Mason.

"Father said that cannon was dangerous," Harry added.

By this time the crowd had surrounded Peter, who lay so still and looked so white. The Bobbsey boys climbed down from the tree and joined the others.

"He's only unconscious from the shock," spoke up Mr. Mason, who was leaning down very close to Peter. "Stand back, and give him air."

The crowd fell back now, and some of the boys looked around to find the pieces of cannon.

"Don't touch it!" said Tom Mason, as a little fellow attempted to pick up a piece of the old gun. "There might be powder in it half lighted."

Mrs. Burns had run over from her home at the report of the accident, and she was now bathing Peter's face with water from the pond.

"He's subject to fainting spells," she told the frightened people, "and I think he'll be all right when he comes to."

Peter looked around, then sat up and rubbed his eyes.

"Did it go off?" he smiled, remembering the big report.

"Guess it did, and you went off with it," Mr. Mason said. "How do you feel?"

"Oh, I'll be all right when my head clears a bit. I guess I fainted."

"So you did," said Mrs. Burns, "and there's no use scolding you for firing that old gun. Come home now and go to bed; you have had all the fireworks you want for one day."

Quite a crowd followed Peter over to his home, for they could not believe he was not in any way hurt.

"Let us go home," Harry said to his cousin.

"We have to get all our fireworks ready before evening."

The boys found all at home enjoying themselves. Freddie's torpedoes still held out, and Flossie had a few more "snakes" left. Nan had company on the lawn, and it indeed was an ideal Fourth of July.

"Look at the balloon!" called John from the carriage house. "It's going to land in the orchard." This announcement caused all the children to hurry up to the orchard, for everybody likes to "catch" a balloon.

"There's a man in it," John exclaimed as the big ball tossed around in the air.

"Yes, that's the balloon that went up from the farmers' picnic," said Harry.

The next minute a parachute shot out from the balloon, and hanging to it the form of a man could be seen.

"Oh, he'll fall!" cried Freddie, all excited. "Let's catch him—in something!"

"He's all right," John assured the little boy. "That umbrella keeps him from coming down too quickly."

"How does it?" Freddie asked.

"Why, you see, sonny, the air gets under the umbrella and holds it up. The man's weight then brings it down gently."

"Oh, maybe he will let us fly up in it," Freddie remarked, much interested.

"Here he comes! Here he comes!" the boys called, and sure enough the big parachute, with the man dangling on it, was now coming right down—down—in the harvest-apple tree!

"Hello there!" called the man from above, closing the colored umbrella and quickly dropping himself from the low tree.

"Hello yourself!" answered John. "Did you have a nice ride?"

"First class," replied the man with the stars on his shirt. "But I've got a long walk back to the grove. Could I hire a bicycle around here?"

Harry spoke to his father, and then quickly decided to let the balloon man ride his bicycle down to the picnic grounds.

"You can leave it at the ice cream stand," Harry told the stranger. "I know the man there, and he will take care of it for me until I call for it."

The children were delighted to talk to a real live man that had been up in a balloon, and the balloonist was indeed very pleasant with the little ones. He took Freddie up in his arms and told him all about how it felt to be up in the sky.

"You're a truly fireman!" Freddie said, after listening to all the dangers there are so far above ground. "I'm a real fireman too!"

Just then the balloon that had been tossing about in the air came down in the other end of the orchard.

"Well, there!" exclaimed the man. "That's good luck. Now, whichever one of you boys gets that balloon first will get ten dollars. That's what we pay for bringing it back!"

With a dash every boy started for the spot where the balloon had landed. There were quite a few others besides the Bobbseys, and they tumbled over each other trying to get there first. Ned Prentice, Nettie's brother, was one of the best runners, and he cut across the orchard to get a clear way out of the crowd.

"Go it, Bert!" called John.

"Keep it up, Harry!" yelled someone else.

"You'll get it, Tom!" came another voice.

But Ned was not in the regular race, and nobody noticed him.

"They've got it," called the excited girls.

"It's Harry!"

"No, it's Bert!"

"'Tisn't either—it's Ned!" called John, as the only poor boy in the crowd proudly touched the big empty gas bag!

"Three cheers for Ned!" called Uncle Daniel, for he and Mr. Bobbsey had joined in the crowd.

"Hurrah! Hurrah! Hurrah!" shouted all the

boys good-naturedly, for Ned was a favorite companion, besides being one who really needed the money.

"Suppose we drive down," Uncle Daniel suggested. "Then we can bring Ned back with his ten dollars."

This was agreed upon as a good plan, and as quickly as John had hitched up the big wagon all the boys piled in with the aeronaut and started for the grove.

CHAPTER 11

THE LITTLE GARDENERS

WHEN little Ned Prentice put the ten-dollar bill in his mother's hand, on that pleasant Fourth of July evening, he felt like a man. His mother could hardly believe the story of Ned's getting the money just for finding a balloon, but when it was explained how valuable the balloon was, and how it sometimes takes days of searching in the woods to find one after the balloonist lets go and drops down with his parachute, she was finally convinced that the money rightfully belonged to Ned.

"No one needs it more than I do," Mrs. Prentice told Mr. Bobbsey, who had brought Ned home in the wagon, "for since the baby was sick we have hardly been able to meet our bills, it cost so much for medicine."

"We were all glad when Ned got there first," Harry said politely, "because we knew he deserved the reward most."

As Ned was a poor boy, and had to work on

farms during vacation, his father being dead and only one brother being old enough to go to work, the reward turned out a great blessing, for ten dollars is a good deal of money for a little boy to earn at one time.

"Be sure to come up to our fireworks tonight," Harry called, as they drove away, and Ned promptly accepted the invitation.

"It has certainly been a great Fourth of July!" Uncle Daniel exclaimed, later in the evening when the children fired off their Roman candles and skyrockets and burned the red fire. The little children had beautiful pinwheels that they put off on the porch. Then Nan had a big fire balloon that she sent up, and they watched it until it was out of sight, away over the pond and clear out of Meadow Brook.

It was a very tired lot of children that rolled off to sleep that night, for indeed it had been a great day for them all.

For a few days after the fourth it rained, as it always does, on account of all the noise that goes up in the air to shake the clouds.

"You can play in the coach house," Aunt Sarah told the children, "but be careful not to run in and out and get wet."

The children promised to remember, and soon they were all out in the big wagon house playing merrily. Freddie climbed in the wagon and made believe it was a "big fire engine." Bert attached a bell on the side for him, and when he pulled a rope this bell would clang like a chemical apparatus. Nan and Flossie had all their dolls in the pretty new carriage with the soft gray cushions, and in this the little girls made believe driving to New York and doing some wonderful shopping.

"Freddie, you be coachman," coaxed Flossie, "because we are inside and have to have someone drive us."

"But who will put out all the fires?" Freddie asked, as he clanged the bell vigorously.

"Make b'lieve they are all out," Flossie told him.

"But you can't make b'lieve about fires," argued the little fellow, "'cause they're really."

"I tell you," Nan suggested. "We will suppose this is a great big high tallyho party, and the ladies always drive them. I'll be away up high on the box, but we ought to have someone blow a horn!"

"I'll blow the horn," Freddie finally gave in, "'cause I got that big fire out now."

So Freddie climbed up on the high coach with his sisters, and blew the horn until Nan told them they had reached New York and were going to stop for dinner.

There were so many splendid things to play

with in the coach house, tables, chairs, and every-thing, that the Bobbseys hardly knew it before it was lunchtime, the morning passed so quickly.

It cleared up in the afternoon and John asked the children if they wanted to help him do some transplanting.

"Oh, we would love to!" Nan answered, for she did love gardening.

The ground was just right for transplanting, after the rain, and the tender little lettuce plants were as easy to take up as they were to put down again.

"I say, Nan," John told her, "you can have that little patch over there for your garden. I'll give you a couple of dozen plants, and we will see what kind of a farmer you will make."

"Oh, thank you, John," Nan answered. "I'll do just as I have seen you doing," and she began to take the little plants in the pasteboard box from one bed to the other.

"Be careful not to shake the dirt off the roots," said John, "and be sure to put one plant in each place. Put them as far apart here as the length of this little stick, and when you put them in the ground press the earth firmly around the roots."

Flossie was delighted to help her sister, and the two girls made a very nice garden indeed.

"Let's put little stones around the path,"

Flossie suggested, and John said they could do this if they would be careful not to let the stones get on the garden.

"I want to be a planter too," called Freddie, running up the path to John. "But I want to plant redishes," he continued, "'cause they're the reddist."

"Well, you just wait a few minutes, sonny," said John, "and I'll show you how to plant radishes. I'll be through with this lettuce in a few minutes."

Freddie waited with some impatience, running first to Nan's garden then back to John's. Finally John was ready to put in a late crop of radishes.

"Now, you see, we make a long drill like this," John explained as he took the drill and made a furrow in the soft ground.

"If it rains again that will be a river," said Freddie, for he had often played river at home after a rain.

"Now, you see this seed is very fine," continued John. "But I am going to let you plant it if you're careful."

"That ain't redishes!" exclaimed Freddie. "I want to plant redishes."

"But this is the seed, and that's what makes the radishes," John explained.

"Nope, that's black and it can't make it red!" argued Freddie.

"Wait and see," the gardener told him. "You

just take this little paper of seeds and scatter them in the drill. See, I have mixed them with sand so they will not grow too thick."

Freddie took the small package, and kneeling down on the board that John used, he dropped the little shower of seeds in the line.

"They're all gone!" he told John presently. "Get some more."

"No, that's enough. Now we will see how your crop grows. See, I just cover the seed very lightly like mamma covers Freddie when he sleeps in the summertime."

"Do you cover them more in the wintertime, too, like mamma does?" Freddie asked.

"Yes, indeed I do," said the gardener, "for seeds are just like babies, they must be kept warm to grow."

Freddie stood watching the line he had planted the seed in.

"They ain't growing yet," he said at last. "Why don't they come up, John?"

"Oh!" laughed the gardener, "they won't come up right away. They have to wake up first. You will see them above the ground in about a week, I guess."

This was rather a disappointment to the little fellow, who never believed in waiting for anything, but he finally consented to let the seeds grow and come back again later to pick the radishes.

"Look at our garden!" called Nan proudly, from across the path. "Doesn't it look straight and pretty?"

"You did very well indeed," said John, inspecting the new lettuce patch. "Now, you'll have to keep it clear of weeds, and if a dry spell should come you must use the watering can."

"I'll come up and tend to it every morning," Nan declared. "I am going to see what kind of lettuce I can raise."

Nan had brought with her a beautiful string of pearl beads set in gold, the gift of one of her aunts. She was very proud of the pearls and loved to wear them whenever her mother would let her.

One afternoon she came to her mother in bitter tears.

"Oh, mamma!" she sobbed. "The—the pearls are gone!"

"Gone! Did you lose them?" questioned Mrs. Bobbsey quickly.

"Yes."

"Where?"

"I—I don't know," and now Nan cried harder than ever.

The news soon spread that the string of pearls were lost, and everybody set to work hunting for them.

"Where do you think you lost 'em?" asked Bert.

"I—I don't know. I was down in the garden, and up the lane, and at the well, and out in the barn, and over to the apple orchard, and feeding the chickens, and over in the hayfield, and—lots of places."

"Then it will be like looking for a needle in a haystack," declared Aunt Sarah.

All the next days the boys and girls hunted for the string of pearls, and the older folks helped. But the string could not be found. Nan felt very bad over her loss, and her mother could do little to console her.

"I—I sup—suppose I'll never see them again," sobbed the girl.

"Oh, I guess they'll turn up some time," said Bert hopefully.

"They can't be lost so very, very bad," lisped Flossie. "'Cause they are somewhere on this farm, ain't they?"

"Yes, but the farm is so very big!" sighed poor Nan.

For a few days Freddie went up to the garden every morning to look for radishes. Then he gave up and declared he knew John had made a mistake and that he didn't plant radishes at all. Nan and Flossie were very faithful attending to their garden, and the beautiful light green lettuce grew splendidly, being grateful for the good care given it.

"When can we pick it?" Nan asked John, as the leaves were getting quite thick.

"In another week!" he told the girls, and so they continued to watch for weeds and kept the ground soft around the plants as John had told them.

Freddie's radishes were above ground now, and growing nicely, but they thought it best not to tell him, as he might pull them up too soon. Nan and Flossie weeded his garden as well as their own and showed they loved to see things grow, for they did not mind the work of attending to them.

"Papa will come up from Lakeport tonight," Nan told Flossie, "and won't he be pleased to see our gardens!"

That evening when Mr. Bobbsey arrived the first thing he had to do was to visit the garden.

"Why, I declare!" he exclaimed in real surprise. "You have done splendidly. This is a fine lettuce patch."

Mrs. Bobbsey and Aunt Sarah had also come up to see the girls' garden, and they too were much surprised at the result of Nan's and Flossie's work.

"Oh!" screamed Freddie from the other side of the garden. "See my redishes! They growed!" and before anyone could stop him he pulled up a whole handful of the little green leaves with the tiny red balls on the roots.

"They growed! They growed!" he shouted, dancing around in delight.

"But you must only pick the ripe ones," his father told him. "And did you really plant them?" Mr. Bobbsey asked in surprise.

"Yep! John showed me," he declared, and the girls said that was really Freddie's garden.

"Now I'll tell you," Aunt Sarah remarked. "We will let our little farmers pick their vegetables for dinner, and then we will be able to say just how good they are."

At this the girls started in to pick the very biggest heads of lettuce, and Freddie looked carefully to get the very reddest radishes in his patch. Finally enough were gathered, and down to the kitchen the vegetables were carried.

"You will have to prepare them for the table," Mrs. Bobbsey said. "Let us see, girls, what a pretty dish you can make."

This was a pleasant task to Nan and Flossie, who both always loved to play at housekeeping, and when at last Nan brought the dish in to the dinner table everybody said how pretty it looked.

"Them's my redishes!" exclaimed Freddie, as he saw the pretty bright red buttons peeping out from between the lettuce leaves.

"But we can all have some, can't we, Freddie?" his father asked.

"Yes, 'course you can. But I don't want all my good redishes smothered in that big dish of green stuff," he pouted.

"Now, Nan, you can serve your vegetables," Aunt Sarah said, and then Nan very neatly put a few crisp lettuce leaves on each small plate, and at the side she placed a few of Freddie's radishes, "with handles on" as Dinah said, meaning the little green stalks.

"Just think, we've done it all from the garden to the table!" Nan exclaimed, justly proud of her success at gardening.

"I done the radishes," put in Freddie, gulping down a drink of water to wash the bite off his tongue, for his radishes were quite hot.

"Well, you have certainly all done very nicely," Mrs. Bobbsey said. "And that kind of play is like going to school, for it teaches you important lessons in nature."

The girls declared they were going to keep a garden all summer, and so they did.

It was an unusually warm night, and so nearly all the doors were left open when the folks went to bed. Freddie was so worked up over his success as a gardener he could not go to sleep.

At last he dozed off, but presently he awoke with a start. What was that strange sound ringing in his ears? He sat up and listened.

Yes, somebody must surely be playing the piano. But what funny music! It seemed to come in funny runs and curious thumps. He called out sharply, and his mother came at once to his side.

"I heard piano playing," said Freddie, and Mrs. Bobbsey started, for she remembered how Flossie had once told her the same thing.

"Oh, Freddie, are you sure?" she asked.

"Sure," repeated the little fellow. "But it wasn't very good playing."

Mrs. Bobbsey called Uncle Daniel, and the latter lit a lamp and went below into the parlor. Nobody was at the piano or in the room.

"I've made a careful examination," he said, on coming back. "I can see nothing unusual. Some of the children left a piece of cake on the keys of the piano, that's all."

"Well, cake can't play," put in Freddie. "Maybe it was a ghost."

"No, you must have been dreaming," said his mother. "Come, go to sleep," and presently Freddie dropped off. Mrs. Bobbsey was much worried, and the next day the older folks talked the matter over, but nothing became of it.

CHAPTER 12

TOM'S RUNAWAY

"Tom Mason is going to bring his colt out this afternoon," said Harry to Bert, "and we can all take turns trying him."

"Oh, is it that pretty little brown horse I saw in the field back of Tom's home?" asked Bert.

"That's him," Harry replied. "Isn't he a beauty?"

"Yes, I would like first-rate to ride him, but young horses are awful skittish, aren't they?"

"Sometimes, but this one is partly broken. At any rate, we wouldn't have far to fall, for he is a little fellow," said Harry.

So the boys went down to Tom's home at the appointed time, and there they met Jack Hopkins.

"We've made a track around the fields," Tom told his companions, "and we will train him to run around the ring, for father thinks he may be a racehorse some day, he's so swift."

"You may go first," the boys told him, "as he's your horse."

91

"All right!" Tom replied, making for the stake where Sable, the pony, was tied. Sable marched along quietly enough and made no objections to Tom getting on his back. There was no saddle, but just the bit in the horse's mouth and attached to it a short piece of rein.

"Get app, Sable!" called Tom, snapping a small whip at the pony's side.

But instead of going forward the little horse tried to sit down!

"Whoa! Whoa!" called the boys, but Tom clung to Sable's neck and held on in spite of the pony's back being like a toboggan slide.

"Get off there, get off there!" urged Tom, yet the funny little animal only backed down more.

"Light a match and set it under his nose," Harry suggested. "That's the way to make a balky horse go!"

Someone had a match, which was lighted and put where Sable could sniff the sulphur.

"Look out! Hold on, Tom!" yelled the boys all at once, for at that instant Sable bolted off like a deer.

"He's running away!" called Bert, which was plain to be seen, for Tom could neither turn him this way or that, but had all he could do to hold on the frightened animal's neck.

"If he throws him Tom will surely be hurt!"

Harry exclaimed, and the boys ran as fast as they could across the field after the runaway.

"Whoa! Whoa! Whoa!" called everybody after the horse, but that made not the slightest difference to Sable, who just went as if the woods were afire. Suddenly he turned and dashed straight up a big hill and over into a neighbor's cornfield.

"Oh, mercy!" cried Harry, "those people are so mean about their garden, they'll have Tom arrested if there's any corn broken."

Of course it was impossible for a runaway horse to go through a field of corn and do no damage, and Tom realized this too. By this time the dogs were out barking furiously, and altogether there was wild excitement. At one end of the field there was a high board fence.

"If I could only get him there he would have to stop," thought Tom, and suddenly he gave Sable a jerk in that direction.

"Drop off, Tom, drop off!" yelled the boys. "He'll throw you against the fence!"

But at that minute the little horse threw himself against the boards in such a way that Tom slid off, yet held tightly to the reins.

The horse fell, quite exhausted.

As quickly as they could get there the boys came up to help Tom.

"Hurry!" said Harry, "there is scarcely any

corn broken, and we can get away before the Trimbles see us. They're away back in the fields planting late cabbage."

Tom felt hardly able to walk, but he limped along while Harry led Sable carefully between the corn hills. It was only a few feet to the edge of the field, and then they were all safe on the road again.

"Are you hurt?" the boys asked Tom, when finally they had a chance to speak about the runaway.

"I feel as if I had dropped from a balloon on a lot of cobblestones," Tom answered, "but I guess that's only the shaking up I got. That pony certainly can go."

"Yes indeed," Harry admitted. "I guess he doesn't like the smell of sulphur matches. Lucky he was not injured with that fall against the fence."

"I found I had to throw him," Tom said, "and I thought the fence was softer than a tree."

"I suppose we ought to make him run until he is played out," said Bert. "That's the way to cure a horse of running away."

But none of the boys felt like risking their bones even to cure Sable, so the panting animal was led to the stable and for the rest of the day allowed to think over his bad conduct.

But that was not the last of the runaway, for in the evening just after supper old Mr. Trimble paid a visit to Tom's father.

"I came over to tell you what a scallywag of a boy you've got," began the cross old man. "He and a lot of young loafers took a horse and drove him all through my cornfield today, and now you've got to pay the damages."

"My son is not a scallywag," Mr. Mason declared, "and if you call him names like loafer and scallywag I'll make you pay damages."

"Oh, you will, eh?" the other sneered. "Think I'm afraid of an old constable up here, do you?"

"Well now, see here," Mr. Mason said. "Be reasonable and do not quarrel over an accident. If any corn is knocked down we will see what it would cost to replace it. But the boys did not do it purposely, and it was worse for Tom than anybody else, for he's all black and blue from the hard knocks he got."

At this the cross man quieted down and said, well, he would see about it. Mr. Trimble was one of those queer people who believe all a boy is good for is doing mischief and all a boy deserves is scolding or beating. Perhaps this was because he had no sons of his own and therefore had no regard for the sons of other people.

Mr. Mason went directly to the cornfield with

his neighbor. He looked carefully over every hill, and with a spade and hoe he was able to put back into place the few stalks that had been knocked down in Sable's flight.

"There now," said Mr. Mason. "I guess that corn is as good as ever. If it wants any more hoeing Tom will come around in the morning and do it. He is too stiff to move tonight."

So that ended the runaway, except for a very lame boy, Tom Mason, who had to limp around for a day or two from stiffness.

"How would you like to be a jockey!" laughed his companions. "You held on like a champion, but you were not in training for the banging you got."

"Well, I guess Sable will make a fine racehorse," said Tom, "when he's broken. But it will take someone stronger than I am to break him in."

The next afternoon all the boys went fishing. They had been out quite late the night before to find the "night walkers" for bait, as those little worms only come out of the ground after dark. Bert had a new line his father brought from Lakeport, and the other boys had nets and hooks, as most country boys who live near streams are always fond of fishing.

"Let's go over to the cove," Harry said when they all started off. "There's lots of good fish in that dark corner."

So the cove was chosen as a good spot to fish from, and soon the Bobbsey boys and their friends were lying around the edge of the deep clear stream, waiting for a bite.

Bert was the first to jerk his line, and he brought it up with such force that the chub-fish on his hook slapped Harry right in the face!

"Look out!" called Harry, trying to dodge the flapping fish. "Put your catch down. He's a good one, but I don't care about having him kiss me that way again."

All the boys laughed at Bert, who was a green fisherman they said. The fish was really a very nice plump chub and weighed more than a pound. He floundered around in the basket and flapped his tail wildly trying to get away from them.

"I've got one," called Tom next, at the same moment pulling his line and bringing up a pretty little sunfish. Now "sunnies" are not considered good eating, so Tom's catch did not come up to Bert's, but it was put in the basket just the same.

"I'm going out on the springboard," August Stout announced, stepping cautiously out on the board from which good swimmers dived.

"You know you can't swim, August," said Harry, "and if you get a catch and jerk it you'll tumble in."

"Oh! I'll be all right," August answered, lying down flat on the narrow springboard and dropping his line.

For a time all the boys lay watching for a bite. No one spoke, for sometimes they say fish are very sensitive to sound and go in another direction if they hear a voice.

It was a beautiful July day, and perhaps the boys were a little lazy. At any rate, they all became so quiet the little woodpeckers on the trees went on with their work pecking at the tree bark as if no human being was in sight.

Suddenly there was a big splash!

"August!" yelled all the boys at once, for indeed August was gone from the springboard.

"Quick!" called Harry to his companions. "He can't swim."

The next minute the boy in the water came to the top and threw up his arm. But no one was near enough to reach it.

"Strike out, August!" yelled Bert. "We're coming," and one boy after the other dropped in the water now, having thrown off their heavy clothing.

"Oh, where is he?" screamed Bert in terror, for no movement on the water's surface showed them where August was.

"Here!" cried Tom Mason, who was quite a distance out. "Here he is! Help! Come quick!"

No need to urge the boys to hasten, for all realized the danger their companion was in.

"Don't pull down, August," went on Tom. "Try to help yourself, or you'll pull me under." Harry had around his neck a strong piece of rope he picked up as he made a dive into the water.

"Take hold of this," he called to August, "and we can all pull."

As the rope was put in August's hand the other boys all took hold and soon towed the unfortunate boy in.

"He's very weak," said Harry when they pulled August up on the shore. "I guess he has swallowed a lot of water. We better roll him on the grass and work his arms up and down. That will revive him."

August was indeed very weak, and had had a narrow escape. For some time his companions worked over him before he opened his eyes and spoke.

"Oh!" he murmured at last, "I'm so sick!"

"I guess you are, August," said Tom, "but you'll be all right soon." They lifted him carefully under a shady tree and removed his wet clothing.

"I'll run over to Smith's and get him something to wear home," said Harry, who hurried across lots and presently returned with an old suit of clothes. August was able to dress himself now, and as soon as he felt strong enough the boys helped him home.

"You can have my fish, August," said Bert nobly.

"And mine too," Tom added. August did not want to accept the boys' offers at first, but at last they prevailed upon him to do so.

"I think I fell asleep," said he, referring to the accident.

"Guess we all did!" added Harry, "for we only woke up when we heard the splash."

It seems the number of accidents country boys have only make them truer friends, for all the things that happened in Meadow Brook made each boy think more of his companion, both in being grateful for the help given and being glad no dear friend's life was lost.

CHAPTER 13

PICKING PEAS

"MOTHER," said Harry, using that loved name to show that what he was about to say was something important, "Peter Burns is sick. He has not been able to work since the cannon exploded and gave him the shock, and all his peas are spoiling because there's no one to pick them. Mrs. Burns hired some boys yesterday, but they broke down so many vines she had to stop them. Mother, would you mind if Bert and I picked some today? The sun is not hot."

"Why, my dear," replied Aunt Sarah, "it would be very nice of you to help Peter; he has always been a kind neighbor. I don't think it would do you any harm to pick peas on a cool day like this. Bert can ask his mother, and if she is satisfied you can put on your play overalls and go right along."

Both boys were given the desired permission, and when Tom and Jack heard where the

Bobbseys were going they said at once they would go along.

"Are you sure your mother won't mind?" Mrs. Burns asked the boys, knowing Harry's folks did not need the money paid to pick the peas. "Of course I'm very glad to have you if your mothers are satisfied."

Soon each boy had a big basket under his arm, and was off for the beautiful field of soft green peas that stretched along the pond bank at the side of Mrs. Burns' home. Now, peas are quite an expensive vegetable when they come in first, and farmers who have big fields of them depend upon the return from the crop as an important part of the summer's income. But the peas must be picked just as soon as they are ripe, or else they will spoil. This was why Harry got his friends to turn in to help poor Peter Burns.

"I'll go down this row and you take that," suggested Bert to Harry. "Then we can talk to each other without hollering."

"All right," Harry replied, snapping the peas off the vines and dropping them into his basket like a real farmer.

"Let's have a real race," called Tom. "See who gets his basket full first."

"But no skipping for big ones," put in Jack. "You have to pick every ripe one."

The boys all started in at the top of the hill, each working two rows at a time. They were so interested in the race that scarcely a word was spoken. The peas were plentiful and ripe too, so that the baskets were filling up quickly. Mrs. Burns herself was picking, in fact she had been in the field since the very first peep of dawn, and she would be sure to stay out until the darkness would drive her in.

"You are fine pickers," she told the boys, seeing how quickly they worked. "I pay ten cents a basket, you know."

"I guess we can earn a dollar a day at this rate," laughed Tom, whose basket was almost full.

"I'm done," called Jack from his row.

"No, you're not," said Harry, "you have to cover the rim."

"Oh!" exclaimed Jack, who had just slipped between the rows. "Oh, there goes my basket!"

And sure enough the big basket had been upset in Jack's fall, and most of the peas were scattered on the ground.

"Ha, ha!" laughed Bert. "I'm first. My basket is full."

"I'm next!" called Tom, picking his basket up in his arms.

"Well, I'll be the last I guess," laughed Tom, trying hard to pick up the scattered peas.

"There's mine!" called Harry, and now all the boys carried their baskets to the big bag at the end of the field and dumped them in.

"It won't take long to fill the bag," said Harry, "and it will be so good for Peter to have them ready, for tomorrow is market day."

So the boys worked on right along until lunchtime, each having picked four big baskets full. August Stout came along and helped some too, but he could not stay long, as he had to cut some clothes poles for his mother.

"Well, I declare!" said Mrs. Burns, looking at the three full bags the boys had picked. "Isn't that splendid! But I can't pay until Peter comes from market."

"We just did it for fun," answered Harry. "We don't want any pay."

"Indeed you must have forty cents apiece, ten cents a basket," she insisted. "See what a good load you have picked!"

"No, really, Mrs. Burns, mother wouldn't like us to take the money," Harry declared. "We are glad to have helped you, and it was only fun."

Poor Mrs. Burns was so grateful she had to wipe her eyes with her gingham apron.

"Well," she said finally. "There are some people in this world who talk about charity, but a good boy is a gift from heaven," and she said this just like a prayer of blessing on the boys who had helped her.

"The crop would have been spoiled tomorrow," remarked Tom, as he and his companions started up the road. "I'm awfully glad you thought of helping her, Harry."

It seemed all that day everything went right for the boys; they did not have even a single mishap in their games or wanderings. Perhaps it was because they felt so happy over having done a good turn for a poor neighbor.

"Say, fellows," Tom said later, while they sat on the pond bank trying to see something interesting in the cool, clear water, "what do you say if we make up a circus!"

"Fine," the others answered, "but what will be the show?"

"Animals, of course," continued Tom. "We've got plenty around here, haven't we?"

"Well, some," Harry admitted. "There's Sable, for instance."

At this the boys all laughed at Tom, remembering the runaway.

"Well, I could be a cowboy, and ride him just the same," spoke up Tom. "I rode him around the track yesterday, and he went all right. He was only scared with that sulphur match when he ran away."

"A circus would be fine," Bert put in. "We could have Frisky as the Sacred Calf."

"And Snoopy as the Wild Cat," said Harry.

"And two trained goats," August added.

"And a real human bear, 'Teddy,'" suggested Jack.

"Then a cage of pigeons," went on Harry.

"Let's get them all in training," said Tom, jumping up suddenly, anxious to begin the sport.

"I tell you!" Harry planned. "We can each train our own animals and then we can bring them together in a well-organized circus."

"When will we have it?" August asked impatiently.

"About next week," Harry thought, and this was decided upon.

During the interval the boys were so busy training that they had little time for other sports, but the girls found outdoor life quite as interesting as their brothers did, and now made many discoveries in and about the pretty woodlands.

"Oh, we saw the prettiest little rabbits today," Nan told her mother, after a trip in the woods. "Flossie and Freddie were sitting on an old stump when two rabbits ran right across the road in front of them. Freddie ran after them as far as he could go in the brushwood, but of course no one can go as fast as a rabbit."

"And the squirrels," Flossie told them. "I think the squirrels are the prettiest things that live in the woods. They have tails just like mamma's feather boa and they walk sitting up so cute."

"Oh, I think the rabbits are the nicest," lisped Freddie, "'cause they are Bunnies, and Bunnies bring Easter eggs."

"And we have made the loveliest fern garden up back of the swing," said Flossie. "We got a whole basket of ferns in the woods and transplanted them."

"In the center we have some lovely Jack-in-the-pulpits," Nan added. "Some are light green striped, and the largest are purple with gold stripes. The Jacks stand up straight, just like real live boys preaching in a pulpit."

"Don't you think, mamma," asked Flossie, "that daisies and violets make a lovely garden? I have a round place in the middle of our wild flower bed just full of light blue violets and white daisies."

"All flowers are beautiful," their mamma told them, "but I do think with Flossie that daisies and violets are very sweet."

"And, mamma, we got a big piece of the loveliest green moss! It is just like real velvet," said Flossie. "We found a place all covered with it down by the pond, under the dark cedar trees.

Nan said it wouldn't grow in our garden, but I brought some home to try. I put it in a cool dark place, and I'm going to put lots of water on it every day."

"Moss must be very cool and damp to grow," Mrs. Bobbsey replied. "I remember how disappointed I used to be when I was a little girl and tried to make it grow around my geraniums. It would always dry up and turn brown in a few days."

"Oh," called Freddie from his garden under the cherry tree, "come quick! Look at the funny bugs!"

Nan and Flossie hurried to where their little brother had dug a hole in the earth.

"They're mice!" exclaimed Nan. "Oh, aren't they cute! Let's catch them. Call Bert or Harry."

While Flossie ran to tell Bert, Nan watched the tiny mice so that they would not get away.

"It's a nest of field mice," Harry told them. "We'll put them in a cage and have them in our circus."

"But they're my mice," cried Freddie, "and I won't let anybody have them!"

"We're only going to help you take care of them in a little box. Oh, there's the mother—catch her, Harry," called Bert.

The mother mouse was not so easy to catch,

however, and the boys had quite a chase after her. At last she ran into a tin box the boys had sunk in the ground when playing golf. Here Harry caught the frightened little creature.

"I've got a queer kind of a trap," Harry said. "It's just like a cage. We can put them in this until we build a larger one. We can make one out of a box with a wire door."

The mice were the smallest, cutest things, not larger than Freddie's thumb. They hardly looked like mice at all, but like some queer little bugs. They were put in the cage trap, mother and all, and then Bert got them a bit of cheese from the kitchen.

"What! Don't feed the mice!" exclaimed Dinah.

"We'll keep them away from the house," Bert told Dinah. "We're going to have a circus, you know, and these will be our trained mice."

Freddie, of course, was delighted with the little things, and wanted to dig for more.

"I tell you!" said Bert. "We might catch butterflies and have them under a big glass on the table with all the small animals."

"That would be good," Harry agreed. "We could catch some big brown ones and some little fancy ones. Then after dark we could get some big moths down by the post office electric light."

The girls, too, went catching butterflies. Nan was able to secure four or five yellow ones in the flower garden near the porch, and Flossie got two of the small brown variety in the nasturtium bed. Harry and Bert searched in the close syringa bushes where the nests are usually found.

"Oh, look at this one!" called Freddie, coming up with a great green butterfly. "Is it a bird?" he asked. "See how big it is!"

It really was very large, and had such beautiful wings it might easily be mistaken for some strange bird.

"We will try to keep them alive," said Harry, "and perhaps we can get ma's big glass globe to put them in. She has one she used to put wax flowers under."

"And, oh say!" exclaimed Bert. "Couldn't we have an aquarium with snakes and turtles and toads in?"

"Fine!" declared Harry. "We've got a big glass tank I used to have goldfish in. We'll get the other fellows to help catch some snakes, fish, and turtles and toads, and—and anything else that will stand water!"

Then what a time they had hunting for reptiles! It seemed each boy had a different variety on his premises. August Stout brought three turtles and Jack Hopkins caught two snakes under a big stone in his backyard. Tom Mason supplied four lovely goldfish, while Ned Prentice brought three bright green frogs.

"I can catch hop-toads," declared Freddie, and sure enough the little fellow brought two big ones and a baby toad in his hat down to the boys, who had their collection in a glass tank in the barn.

"We can't put the snakes in with the others or they'll eat them up," said Jack. "I'll get a big glass jar for the snakes."

"And say!" said Harry. "Will we charge admission to the show?"

"Sure—five cents each," said Tom, "and give the money to the fresh-air camp over on the mountain."

This was considered a good plan, and now it was only a few days more until Wednesday—the day of the circus!

CHAPTER 14

THE CIRCUS

NEWS of the circus had spread from one end of Meadow Brook to the other. Every boy and girl in the place expected to get in to see the sights, and even some grown folks had made up their minds, from what they heard, there would be something interesting for them to see, and so they decided to go too.

Mrs. Bobbsey, Aunt Sarah, Dinah, and Martha had bought tickets for reserved seats (these cost ten cents each). Then Mildred Manners was going to bring her mother and her big sister, and Mabel Herold expected to have her mother with her also. Mr. Bobbsey was coming up from Lakeport purposely to see the circus, and Uncle Daniel had helped the boys put up the seats and fix things generally. A big tent had been borrowed from the Herolds; they were only out at Meadow Brook for the summer, and this tent was erected in the open field between the Bobbsey and the

Mason farms, alongside the track where Tom had tried Sable.

The tent had large flaps that opened up the entire front, so that all the exhibits could be shown nicely to the people on the seats outside.

The seats were made of boards set on most anything that would hold them, with a few garden benches for reserved seats at the front.

Everything was ready, and the circus day came at last.

"Lucky it isn't raining," the boys declared, as they rushed around putting the final touches to everything.

August Stout was appointed to collect the tickets, and Ned Prentice was to show the people to their seats.

Two o'clock!

Only one hour more!

Lots of children came early to get good seats. Roy Mason sat right in the front row alongside of Freddie. Nettie Prentice was on the very first bench back of the reserved seats. The Herolds came next, and had Aunt Sarah's front garden bench, the red one. Mildred Manners' folks paid ten cents each too, and they had the big green bench from the side porch.

"Give Mrs. Burns a front seat," Harry whispered to Ned, as the busy farmer's wife actually stopped her work to see what all the excitement was about.

The Bobbseys had come—Mr. Bobbsey and all—and Dinah wore her best bonnet.

"When will it begin?" Flossie asked, just trembling with excitement.

"I saw Harry and Bert go in the tent some time ago," whispered Nan. "And see, they are loosing the tent flap."

There was a shout of applause when Harry appeared. He actually wore a swallowtail coat and had on a choker—a very high collar—and a bright green tie. He wore long trousers too, and looked so queer even Aunt Sarah had to laugh when she saw him.

"Oh!" exclaimed all the children when they looked inside the tent.

"Isn't it grand!" whispered Flossie.

Then Bert stepped up on the soap box in the middle of the ring.

"Ladies and gentlemen," he began, making a profound bow, "ladies and gentlemen—"

Then everybody roared laughing.

Bert had to wait until they got through laughing at his funny costume, which was a good deal like Harry's, only the latter wore a red tie. In a few moments Bert went on again.

"Ladies and gentlemen! Our first number is

Frisky, the Sacred Calf of India!" he exclaimed, imitating that queer-voiced man called a "Barker" and used at circuses.

Snap! snap! went Bert's whip, and out from a side place, back of a big screen, came Jack Hopkins dressed like a real clown, leading our old friend Frisky, the runaway calf.

How awfully funny it was!

The calf had over him a plush portière that reached clear down to the ground, and over each ear was tied a long-handled feather duster!

Such laughing and clapping as greeted this "first number"!

Frisky just turned around square in front and looked the people straight in the face. This funny move made Mr. Bobbsey "die laughing," as Flossie said, and Uncle Daniel too was hilarious.

"The sacred calf is too sacred to smile," laughed Uncle Daniel, while Dinah and Martha just roared.

The children didn't think they ought to laugh out loud and spoil the show; even Freddie raised his finger to Dinah.

Suddenly the clown jumped on the calf's back. He tried to stand on his head. Then he turned a somersault on to the sawdust.

Everybody clapped hard now, and the children began to shout.

But Bert snapped his whip and the clown went down on his hands and knees to apologize. Of course clowns are not supposed to speak, so Jack did everything by pantomime.

Next he came around and kissed Frisky. This made everybody roar again, and no matter what the clown did it certainly looked very funny.

Finally Bert snapped his whip three times, and the clown jumped on Frisky's back, over the plush curtain and all, and rode off.

"Wasn't that splendid!" everybody exclaimed.

"I really never enjoyed a big circus more than this!" remarked Mrs. Bobbsey to Mrs. Burns. The others all said nice things too; and then Bert announced the next turn.

"Ladies and gentlemen," he began again, "our next number will introduce to you the famous wildcats, Snoop and Fluffy. Real wildcats from the jungle, and this is the first—time—they—have ever been—exhibited in—this country!"

Snap went the whip, and out came Harry with our little kitten friends one on each arm.

He whistled, and Snoop climbed on his shoulder!

He whistled again, and Fluffy climbed on the other shoulder.

This "brought the house down," as Uncle Daniel said, and there was so much noise the kittens looked frightened.

Next Harry stretched out both arms straight and the kittens carefully walked over into his hands.

"Well, I declare!" exclaimed. "Look at Snoop!"

"And look at Fluffy!" exclaimed Martha. "As white as Snoop is black!" Harry stooped down and let the kittens jump through his hands, which is an old but nonetheless very pretty trick.

With the air of a real master, Bert snapped his whip and placed on the table a little piece of board. He rubbed something on each end (it was a bit of dried herring, but the people didn't know that), then Harry put Snoop on one end and Fluffy on the other.

"Oh, a teeter-totter!" called Freddie, unable to restrain his joy any longer. "I bet on Snoop. He's the heaviest."

At the sound of Freddie's voice Snoop turned around and the move sent Fluffy up in the air.

"Oh, oh, oh!" came a chorus from the children, but before anybody in the circus had time to interfere off went Fluffy, as hard as she could run, over the lots, home.

The next minute Snoop was after her, and Harry stood alone in the ring bowing to the "tremendous applause."

When the laughing had ceased Bert made the next announcement.

"Ladies and gentlemen," he said, "we will now introduce our famous menagerie. First we have the singing mice."

"They're mine!" called Freddie, but Nan insisted on him keeping quiet.

"Now you will hear the mice sing," said Bert, and as he held up the cage of little mice somebody whistled a funny tune back of the scenes.

"Good, good!" called Mr. Bobbsey. "We've got real talent here," he added, for indeed the boys had put together a fine show.

"Now you see our aquarium," went on Bert as Harry helped him bring forward the table that held the glass tank.

"Here we have a real sea serpent," he said, pointing to a good fat chub that flopped around in the water.

"Let the little ones walk right up and see them," Bert said. "Form in line and pass in this way."

Not only the children went up, but grown folks too, for they wanted a look into the tank.

"Now here are our alligators and crocodiles," announced Bert, pointing his whip at the turtles.

"And these are sea lions," he said, pointing out Freddie's hop-toads.

At each announcement everybody laughed, but Bert went on as seriously as if he were deaf.

"In this separate tank," he declared, "we have our boa constrictors, the largest and fiercest in the world. This is the first time one of this specimen has ever been captured alive. Note the dangerous stripe on his back!"

It was Jack's snakes that came in for this description, and the girls were quite afraid of them, although they were in a glass jar.

"Well, I declare!" said Mrs. Burns. "If this isn't a sure-enough circus. I often paid a half-dollar when I went to see things no better than these!"

Everybody thought everything was splendid, and the boys were well paid for their efforts.

"Now," said Bert, "here are our crystal fish from the deep sea!" (These were Tom's goldfish.) "You will notice how bespangled they are. They say this comes from the fish eating the diamonds lost in shipwrecks."

"What a whopper!" called someone back of the scenes whose voice sounded like Tom Mason's.

Snap! went Bert's whip, and the boys did not interrupt him again.

"The last part of our menagerie is the cage of prize butterflies," said Bert. "These butterflies are rare and scarce and—"

"Hard to catch!" remarked someone not on the programme.

"Now there will be a ten-minute intermission,"

the announcer said, "so all may have time to see everything in the menagerie.

"After that we will give you the best number of the programme, our chariot race."

"Oh, that's going to be Tom!" exclaimed Roy.

"No, it's Bert," said Flossie.

"Well, Jack has our goat wagon," said Mildred.

"I guess there'll be a whole lot in the race," said Freddie, "and maybe they'll have firemen."

During the intermission August sold a whole big basket of peanuts, and the people wanted more. They knew all the money was to go to the fresh-air camp, which was probably the reason they bought so generously.

"I don't know when I have enjoyed myself so much," declared Mrs. Manners, fanning herself. "I had no idea boys could be so clever."

"That's because you only have girls," laughed Mrs. Bobbsey.

"Don't you think we ought to give them a treat for working so hard?" whispered Mrs. Herold to Aunt Sarah. "I would be delighted to have them all to dinner," she added, in her society way, for the Herolds were quite rich.

"That would be very nice, I'm sure," Aunt Sarah replied. "Boys always have good appetites after having a lot of fun."

All this time there was plenty of noise back of

the scenes, and it was evident something big was being prepared.

Presently Bert and Harry came out and lowered the tent flap, first making sure all the little sightseers were outside.

"They're comin'!" exclaimed Freddie, clapping his fat hands.

"Oh, I'm just so nervous!" whispered Flossie. "I hope none of the animals will get loose."

"Now, ladies and gentlemen," called Tom Mason, appearing at the tent, "if you will just turn round the other way in your seats and face that ring we will give you an exhibition of cowboy life on the plains!"

CHAPTER 15

THE CHARIOT RACE

TOM'S costume was a splendid imitation of a cowboy. He wore tan-colored overalls and a jumper, the jumper being slashed up at the sides like an Indian's coat. On his head was a very broad sombrero, this hat having really come from the plains, as it belonged to a Western farmer who had lately moved to Meadow Brook.

Presently Tom appeared again, this time riding the fiery Sable.

"Hurrah, hurrah!" shouted the boys, as Tom drove into the ring like a major.

Bert now stepped into the middle of the ring alongside of some soap boxes that were piled up there.

"Now you see, ladies and gentlemen," began Bert, laughing a little at the show in broad daylight, "you see this (the soap boxes) is a mail coach. Our cowboy will rob the mail coach from his horse just as they used to do in the mountains of Arizona."

Snap went the whip, and away went Sable around the ring at a nice even canter. After a few turns around Tom urged his horse on a little until he was going on a steady run. Everyone kept quiet, for most of Meadow Brook people had heard how Sable had run away some days before.

"There ought to be music," whispered Jack to Harry, for indeed the circus was so real it only lacked a brass band.

Now Bert put on top of the soap boxes Harry's canvas schoolbag stuffed full of papers.

"This is the United States mail," he said. "We will understand that the coach has stopped for a few minutes."

Sable was going along splendidly by this time, and everybody said what a pretty little horse he was.

"He's goin' to steal the mailbox now!" whispered Flossie to Freddie. "I hope Sable won't fall or anything."

Snap! snap! went the whip as the horse ran faster and faster.

All of a sudden Tom got a good tight hold on the reins, then he pulled up alongside of the mail coach, leaned over, grabbed the mail bag, and turned his horse at full speed around the ring.

"Hurrah, hurrah!" shouted everybody.

"Well done!" called Uncle Daniel.

"Couldn't be better!" exclaimed Mr. Bobbsey.

Tom waved his hat now and patted Sable affectionately, as all good riders do when their horses have done well in the ring.

The men admired the little horse so much they came up and asked the "cowboy" a lot of questions about him, how old he was and who broke him in.

"One more number," called Bert. "The chariot race."

At this all took their seats again, and out trotted two clowns, Jack and August, each riding in a little goat wagon.

The goats were decorated with the Fourth of July buntings and the wagons had the tailboards out and were tipped up like circus chariots.

The clowns pulled up in line.

"One, two, three!" called Bert, with a really big revolver up in the air.

"Ready! Set! Go!" Bang went the revolver (a blank cartridge, of course) and away started the chariots.

Jack wore a broad green belt and August had yellow. Jack darted ahead!

"Go it, green!" shouted one group of boys.

"Pass him, orange!" called another crowd.

Now August passed Jack just as they crossed the line.

"One!" called Bert. "We will have ten rounds."

In the next the wagons kept almost even until just within a few feet of the line, then Jack crossed first.

"Two!" called Bert, while all the boys shouted for their favorites.

In the next three or four turns the riders divided even. Finally the last round was reached and the boys had tied; that is, both were even when the round started. This of course made the race very interesting, as both had equal chances of winning.

"I'll put a dollar on green," called Mr. Bobbsey. "For the fresh-air fund."

"I'll put one on orange," called Uncle Daniel, "for the same charity."

Then the ladies all wanted to bet, but Bert said it was against the rules to allow betting.

"We will take all the money you want to give us," said Bert, "but we cannot allow betting on the races."

"All ready!" called the ringmaster, holding his revolver high in the air again.

Bang went the gun!

Off went the chariots!

My, how those little goats did run!

"Go it, green!"

"Go it, orange!"

Shout after shout greeted the riders as they urged their steeds around the ring.

Suddenly Jack's chariot crossed in front of August.

"Foul!" called Bert, while Jack tried his best to get on his own side again.

"Back! Back!" yelled Jack to his horse (goat), but the little animal was too excited to obey.

Finally fat August Stout, the funniest clown, dashed home first and won the race!

"Hurrah for Nero!" called everybody. "Hurrah, hurrah, hurrah!" shouted the boys long and loud.

The circus was over!

The money was counted, and there was exactly twenty-three dollars to be given to the poor children in the Meadow Brook Fresh-Air Camp.

Wasn't that splendid? And to think everybody had such a good time too!

Freddie and Roy were allowed to ride home in the goat wagons, and they tried to race along the way.

A committee of five boys, Bert, Harry, Jack, Tom, and August, took the money over to the fresh-air camp the next day, and the managers said it was a very welcome gift, for new coats were needed for some sick children that were expected to come out from the city as soon as provision could be made for them.

"Somebody dropped a two-dollar bill in the ticket box," August told his companions. "Then there were the other two dollars from the race, besides some fifty-cent pieces I don't know who gave. Of course we couldn't make all that just on five- and ten-cent seats. And I took in two dollars on the peanuts besides."

"Well, we're all satisfied," said Harry. "And I guess everybody had a good time."

"Sure they did," spoke up Tom, "and I hope Bert will come out here next year to help us with another big circus. They're the best fun we ever had."

For some days every boy and girl in Meadow Brook talked about the circus, which had really been a greater success than even the boys themselves had expected.

It was a warm afternoon quite late in July—one of those days that make a boy feel lazy and inclined to stretch himself.

Bert and Harry were down back of the barn sitting on the fresh stack of hay that had just been piled up by John the stableman.

"Did you ever try smoking?" Harry asked Bert suddenly, as if he had discovered something new and interesting.

"No!" answered Bert in surprise. "Father wouldn't let me smoke."

"Neither would pa," said Harry, "but I suppose every fellow has to try it some time. I've seen them make cigarettes out of corn silk."

"I suppose that is not as bad as tobacco," replied Bert.

"No," answered Harry, "there's no harm in corn silk. Guess I'll try to roll a cigarette."

At this Harry slid down off the hay and pulled from the fast withering corn some dry silk. With a good handful he went back to Bert.

"I've got some soft paper," he said, sitting down again and beginning the task.

Bert watched with interest, but really had no idea of doing wrong.

"There!" exclaimed Harry, giving the ends of the cigarette a twist. "How is that?"

"Pretty good," answered Bert. "Looks like a real one."

"Let's try it!" went on Harry.

"Not in the hay," exclaimed Bert. "You might drop the match."

At this Harry slid down along the side of the stack, and Bert followed.

It did seem wrong as soon as Harry struck the match, but the cigarette being only corn silk made the boys forget all the warnings never to smoke.

Harry gave a puff or two. Then he choked a little.

"Kinder strong," he spluttered. "You try it!"

Bert put the cigarette in his mouth. He drew it once or twice, then quickly tossed it aside.

"Ouch!" he exclaimed. "Tastes like old shoes!"

At that time John came up and piled on some more hay. The boys of course had to act as if nothing had happened, and dared not look around to find the lighted cigarette, even though they wanted to very much.

"I hope it went out," Bert said, as John walked away again.

"If it didn't it's under the hay," said Harry, somewhat alarmed. "But I guess it's out."

"My, look at the storm coming!" Bert exclaimed suddenly. "We ought to help John with that load of hay."

"All right," said Harry, "come along!" and with this the two boys started on a run down through the fields into the open meadow, where the dry hay was being packed up ready to put on the hay rick.

John, of course, was very glad of the help, for it spoils hay to get it wet, so all three worked hard to load up before the heavy shower should come up.

"All ready!" called John, "and no time to lose."

At this the boys jumped up and all started for the barn.

"There's smoke!" exclaimed Harry in terror as they neared the barn.

"The barn is afire!" screamed John the next minute, almost falling from his seat on the wagon in his haste to get down.

"Quick! Quick!" yelled the boys, so frightened they could hardly move.

"The hose!" called John, seeing flames now shoot out of the barn windows. "Get the hose, Harry; it's in the coach house. I'll get a bucket while you attach the hose."

By this time everybody was out from the house.

"Oh, mercy!" cried Aunt Sarah. "Our whole barn will be burned."

Uncle Daniel was with John now, pouring water on the flames that were gaining in spite of all efforts to put them out.

"Where's the firemen!" cried little Freddie, in real tears this time, for he, like all the others, was awfully frightened.

The boys had a stream from the hose now, but this too was of no account, for the flames had shot up from the big pile of dry hay!

"The firemen!" called Freddie again.

"There are no firemen in the country, Freddie," Nan told him. "We have to put the fire out ourselves."

"We can't then," he went on, "and all the other barns will burn too."

There was indeed great danger, for the flames were getting ahead rapidly.

All this time the terrific thunderstorm was coming up.

Clap after clap of thunder rolled over the hills and made the fire look more terrible against the black sky.

"The rain!" exclaimed Uncle Daniel at last. "The rain may put it out; we can't."

At this one terrific clap of thunder came. Then the downpour of rain. It came like a very deluge, and as it fell on the flames it sent out steam and smoke but quickly subdued the cracking and flashing of the fire.

Everybody ran to the back porch now but John and Uncle Daniel. They went in the coach house at the side of the barn.

"How could it have caught fire?" Aunt Sarah said. But Harry and Bert were both very pale, and never said a word.

How heavily the rain did pour down, just like a cloudburst! And as it struck the fire even the smoke began to die out.

"It's going out!" exclaimed Harry. "Oh, I hope it keeps on raining!"

Soon there was even no more smoke!

"It's out!" called John, a little later. "That was a lucky storm for us."

CHAPTER 16

THE FLOOD

THE heavy downpour of rain had ceased now, and everybody ran to the barn to see what damage the fire had done.

"It almost caught my pigeon coop!" said Harry, as he examined the blackened beams in the barn near the wire cage his birds lived in.

"The entire back of this barn will have to be rebuilt," said Uncle Daniel. "John, are you sure you didn't drop a match in the hay?"

"Positive, sir!" answered John. "I never use a match while I'm working. Didn't even have one in my clothes."

Bert whispered something to Harry. It was too much to have John blamed for their wrongdoing.

"Father!" said Harry bravely, but with tears in his eyes. "It was our fault. We set the barn afire!"

"What!" exclaimed Uncle Daniel in surprise. "You boys set the barn afire!"

"Yes," spoke up Bert. "It was mostly my fault.

I threw the cigarette away and we couldn't find it."

"Cigarette!" exclaimed Uncle Daniel. "What!—you boys smoking!"

Both Bert and Harry started to cry. They were not used to being spoken to like that, and of course they realized how much it cost to put that nasty old cigarette in their mouths. Besides there might have been a great deal more damage if it hadn't been for the rain.

"Come with me!" Uncle Daniel said. "We must find out how all this happened," and he led the unhappy boys into the coach house, where they all sat down on a bench.

"Now, Harry, stop your crying, and tell me about it," the father commanded.

Harry tried to obey, but his tears choked him. Bert was the first able to speak.

"Oh, Uncle Daniel," he cried, "we really didn't mean to smoke. We only rolled up some corn silk in a piece of paper and—and—"

His tears choked back his words now, and Harry said:

"It was I who rolled the cigarette, father, and it was awful, it almost made us sick. Then when Bert put it in his mouth—"

"I threw it away and it must have fallen in the hay!" said Bert.

"Why didn't you come and tell me?" questioned Uncle Daniel severely. "It was bad enough to do all that, but worse to take the risk of fire!"

"Well, the storm was coming," Harry answered, "and we went to help John with the hay!"

"Now, boys," said Uncle Daniel, "this has been a very serious lesson to you and one that you will remember all your lives. I need not punish you any more. You have suffered enough from the fright of that awful fire. And if it hadn't been that you were always pretty good boys the Lord would not have sent that shower to save us as He did."

"I'll bet I'll never smoke again as long as I live," said Harry determinedly through his tears.

"Neither will I," said Bert firmly, "and I'll try to make other fellows stop if I can."

"All right," answered Uncle Daniel, "I'm sure you mean that, and don't forget to thank the Lord tonight for helping us as He did. And you must ask His pardon too for doing wrong, remember."

This ended the boys' confession, but they could not stop crying for a long time, and Bert felt so sick and nervous he went to bed without eating any supper. Uncle Daniel gave orders that no one should refer to the fire or cause the boys any more worry, as they were both really very nervous from the shock, so that beyond helping John clear things up in the burned end of the barn, there was no further reference to the boys' accident.

Next day it rained very hard—in fact, it was one of those storms that come every summer and do not seem to know when to go away.

"The gate at the sawmill dam is closed," Harry told Bert, "and if the pond gets any higher they won't be able to cross the plank to open up the gate and let the water out."

"That would be dangerous, wouldn't it?" Bert asked.

"Very," replied Harry. "Peter Burns' house is right in line with the dam at the other side of the plank, and if the dam should ever burst that house would be swept away."

"And the barn and henhouse are nearer the pond than the house even!" Bert remarked. "It would be an awful loss for a poor man."

"Let's go up in the attic and see how high the pond is," Harry suggested.

From the top of the house the boys could see across the high pond bank into the water.

"My!" Bert exclaimed. "Isn't it awful!"

"Yes, it is," Harry replied. "You see, all the streams from the mountains wash into this pond, and in a big storm like this it gets very dangerous."

"Why do they build houses in such dangerous places?" asked Bert.

"Oh, you see, the Burns house has stood there

maybe one hundred years—long before any dam was put in the pond to work the sawmill," said Harry.

"Oh, that's it—is it?" Bert replied. "I thought it was queer to put houses right in line with a dam."

"See how strong the water is getting," went on Harry. "Look at that big log floating down."

"It will be fun when it stops raining," remarked Bert. "We can sail things almost anywhere."

"Yes, I've seen the pond come right up across the road down at Hopkins' once," Harry told his cousin. "That was when it had rained a whole week without stopping."

"Say," called Dinah from the foot of the stairs. "You boys up there better get your boots on and look after that Frisky cow. John's gone off somewhere, and that calf is crying herself sick out in the barn. Maybe she's drowning."

It did not take long to get their boots and overcoats on and hurry out to the barn.

"Sure enough, she is getting drowned!" exclaimed Harry, as they saw the poor little calf standing in water up to her knees.

"Where is all the water coming from?" asked Bert.

"I don't know," Harry answered, "unless the tank upstairs has overflowed."

The boys ran up the stairs and found, just as Harry thought, the tank that supplied all the barns with water, and which also gave a supply for the house to be used on the lawn, was flowing over.

"Is there any way of letting it out?" asked Bert, quite frightened.

"We can open all the faucets, besides dipping out pailfuls," said Harry. "But I wish John would get back."

Harry ran to get the big water pail, while Bert turned on the faucet at the outside of the barn, the one in the horse stable, another that supplied water for the chickens and ducks, and the one John used for carriage washing. Frisky, of course, had been moved to a dry corner and now stopped crying.

Harry gathered all the large water pails he could carry, and hurried up to the tank followed by Bert.

"It has gone down already," said Harry, as they looked into the tank again. "But we had better dip out all we can, to make sure. Lucky we found it as soon as we did, for there are all father's tools on the bench right under the tank, besides all those new paints that have just been opened."

"Here comes John now," said Bert, as he heard the barn door open and shut again.

"Come up here, John!" called Harry. "We're almost flooded out. The tank overflowed."

"It did!" exclaimed John. "Gracious! I hope nothing is spoiled."

"Oh, we caught it just in time," Harry told him, "and we opened up the faucets as soon as we could. Then we began dipping out, to make sure."

"You were smart boys this time," John told him, "and saved a lot of trouble by being so prompt to act. There is going to be a flood sure. The dam is roaring like Niagara, and they haven't opened the gates yet."

"I'm glad we are up high," Bert remarked, for he had never seen a country flood before, and was a good deal frightened at the prospect.

"Hey, John!" called Freddie from the back porch. "Hey, bring me some more nails, will you? I need them for my ark."

"He's building an ark!" laughed Bert. "Guess we'll need it all right if this keeps on."

Harry got some nails from his toolbox in the carriage house, and the boys went up to the house.

There they found Freddie on the hard cement cellar floor, nailing boards together as fast as his little hammer could drive the nails in.

"How's that?" asked the little fellow, standing up the raft.

"I guess that will float," said Bert, "and when it stops raining we can try it."

"I'm going to make a regular ark like the play one I've got home," said Freddie, "only mine will be a big one with room for us all, besides Frisky, Snoop, Fluffy, and—"

"Old Bill. We'll need a horse to tow us back when the water goes down," laughed Harry.

Freddie went on working as seriously as if he really expected to be a little Noah and save all the people from the flood.

"My, but it does rain!" exclaimed somebody on the front porch.

It was Uncle Daniel, who had just returned from the village, soaking wet.

"They can't open the gates," Uncle Daniel told Aunt Sarah. "They let the water get so high the planks sailed away and now they can't get near the dam."

"That is bad for the poor Burns family!" exclaimed Aunt Sarah. "I had better have John drive me down and see if they need anything."

"I stopped in on my way up," Uncle Daniel told her, "and they were about ready to move out. We'll bring them up here if it gets any worse."

"Why don't they go to the gates in a boat?" asked Bert.

"Why, my dear boy," said Uncle Daniel, "anybody who would go near that torrent in a boat might as well jump off the bridge. The falls are twenty-five feet high, and the water seems to have built them up twice that. If one went within two hundred feet of the dam the surging water would carry him over."

"You see," said Harry, explaining it further, "there is like a window in the falls, a long low door. When this is opened the water is drawn down under and does not all have to go over the falls."

"And if there is too much pressure against the stone wall that makes the dam, the wall may be carried away. That's what we call the dam bursting," finished Uncle Daniel.

All this was very interesting to Bert, who could not help being frightened at the situation.

The boys told Uncle Daniel how the tank in the barn had overflowed, and he said they had done good work to prevent any damage.

"Oh, Uncle Daniel!" exclaimed Freddie, just then running up from the cellar. "Come and see my ark! It's most done, and I'm going to put all the animals and things in it to save them from the flood."

"An ark!" exclaimed his uncle, laughing. "Well, you're a sensible little fellow to build an ark today, Freddie, for we will surely need one if this keeps up," and away they went to examine the raft Freddie had actually nailed together in the cellar.

That was an awful night in Meadow Brook, and few people went to bed, staying up instead to watch the danger of the flood. The men took turns walking along the pond bank all night long, and their low call each hour seemed to strike terror in the hearts of those who were in danger.

The men carried lanterns, and the little specks of light were all that could be seen through the darkness.

Mrs. Burns had refused to leave her home.

"I will stay as long as I can," she told Uncle Daniel. "I have lived here many a year, and that dam has not broken yet, so I'm not going to give up hope now!"

"But you could hardly get out in time should it break," insisted Uncle Daniel, "and you know we have plenty of room and you are welcome with us."

Still she insisted on staying, and each hour when the watchman would call from the pond bank, just like they used to do in old wartimes: "Two—o'clock—and—all—is—well!" Mrs. Burns would look up and say, "Dear Lord, I thank Thee!"

Peter, of course, was out with the men. He could not move his barns and chicken house, but he had taken his cow and horse to places of safety.

There were other families along the road in danger as well as the Burnses, but they were not so near the dam, and would get some warning to escape before the flood could reach them should the dam burst.

How the water roared! And how awfully dark it was! Would morning ever come?

"Four o'clock—the water rises!" shouted the men from the bank.

"Here, Mary!" called Peter Burns at the door of their little home, "you put your shawl on and run up the road as fast as you can! Don't wait to take anything, but go!"

"Oh, my babies' pictures!" she cried. "My dear babies! I must have them."

The poor frightened little woman rushed about the house looking for the much-prized pictures of her babies that were in heaven.

"It's a good thing they all have a safe home tonight," she thought, "for their mother could not give them safety if they were here."

"Come, Mary," called Peter, outside. "That dam is swaying like a treetop, and it will go over any minute." With one last look at the little home Mrs. Burns went out and closed the door.

Outside there were people from all along the road. Some driven out of their homes in alarm, others having turned out to help their neighbors.

The watchmen had left the bank. A torrent from the dam would surely wash that away, and brave as the men were they could not watch the flood any longer.

"Get past the willows quick!" called the men. "Let everybody who is not needed hurry up the road!"

Mr. Mason, Mr. Hopkins, Uncle Daniel, and John, besides Peter Burns, were the men most active in the lifesaving work. There were not many boats to be had, but what there were had been brought inland early in the day, for otherwise they would have been washed away long before down the stream into the river.

"What that?" called Uncle Daniel, as there was a heavy crash over near the gates.

Then everybody listened breathless.

It was just coming daylight, and the first streak of dawn saw the end of the awful rain.

Not one man in the crowd dared to run up that pond bank and look over the gates!

"It's pretty strong!" said the watchman. "I expected to hear it crash an hour ago!"

There was another crash!

"There she goes!" said Mr. Burns, and then nobody spoke.

CHAPTER 17

A TOWN AFLOAT

"Is she going?" asked Uncle Daniel at last, after a wait of several minutes.

Daylight was there now, and was ever dawn more welcome in Meadow Brook!

"I'll go up to the pipes," volunteered John. "And I can see from there."

Now, the pipes were great water conduits, the immense black iron kind that are used for carrying water into cities from reservoirs. They were situated quite a way from the dam, but as it was daylight John could see the gates as he stood on the pipes that crossed above the pond.

Usually boys could walk across these pipes in safety, as they were far above the water, but the flood had raised the stream so that the water just reached the pipes, and John had to be careful.

"What's that?" he said, as he looked down the raging stream.

"Something lies across the dam!" he shouted

to the anxious listeners.

This was enough. In another minute every man was on the pond bank.

"The big elm!" they shouted. "It has saved the dam!"

What a wonderful thing had happened! The giant elm tree that for so many, many years had stood on the edge of the stream, was in this great flood washed away, and as it crossed the dam it broke the force of the torrent, really making another waterfall.

"It is safe now!" exclaimed Uncle Daniel in surprise. "It was the tree we heard crash against the bank. The storm is broken at last, and that tree will hold where it is stuck until the force goes down. Then we can open the gates."

To think that the houses were safe again! That poor Mrs. Burns could come back to the old mill home once more!

"We must never have this risk again," said Mr. Mason to Uncle Daniel. "When the water goes down we will open the gates, then the next dry spell that comes when there is little water in the pond we will break that dam and let the water run through in a stream. If the mill people want waterpower they will have to get it some place where it will not endanger lives."

Uncle Daniel agreed with Mr. Mason, and as

they were both town officials, it was quite likely what they said would be done in Meadow Brook.

"Hey, Bert and Harry!" called Tom Mason, as he and Jack Hopkins ran past the Bobbsey place on their way to see the dam. "Come on down and see the flood."

The boys did not wait for breakfast, but with a buttered roll in hand Harry and Bert joined the others and hurried off to the flood.

"Did the dam burst?" was the first question everybody asked along the way, and when told how the elm tree had saved it the people were greatly astonished.

"Look at this," called Tom, as they came to a turn in the road where the pond ran level with the fields. That was where it was only a stream, and no embankment had been built around it.

"Look!" exclaimed Jack. "The water has come up clear across the road, and we can only pass by walking on the high board fence."

"Or get a boat," said Tom. "Let's go back to the turn and see if there's a boat tied anywhere."

"Here's Herolds'," called Harry, as they found the pretty little rowboat, used for pleasure by the summer cottagers, tied up to a tree.

"We'll just borrow that," said Jack, and then the four boys lifted the boat to that part of the road where the water ran.

"All get in, and I'll push off," said Harry, who had hip boots on. The other three climbed in, then Harry gave a good push and scrambled over the edge himself.

"Think of rowing a boat in the middle of a street," said Bert. "That's the way they do in Naples," he added, "but I never expected to see such a thing in Meadow Brook."

The boys pushed along quite easily, as the water was deep enough to use oars in, and soon they had rounded the curve of the road and were in sight of the people looking at the dam.

"What an immense tree!" exclaimed Bert, as they left their boat and mounted the bank.

"That's what saved the dam!" said Harry. "Now Mrs. Burns can come back home again."

"But look there!" called Tom. "There goes Peter Burns' chicken house."

Sure enough, the henhouse had left its foundation and now toppled over into the stream.

It had been built below the falls, near the Burns house, and Peter had some valuable ducks and chickens in it.

"The chickens!" called Jack, as they ran along. "Get the boat, Harry, and we can save some."

The boys were dashing out right now in the stream, Jack and Tom being good oarsmen.

But the poor chickens! What an awful noise

they made, as they tried to keep on the dry side of the floating house!

The ducks, of course, didn't mind it, but they added their queer quacking to the noise.

"We can never catch any of the chickens," said Harry. "We ought to have a rope and pull the house in."

"A rope," called Tom to the crowd on the shore. "Throw us a rope!"

Someone ran off and got one, and it was quickly thrown out to the boys in the boat.

"Push up closer," Tom told Harry and Bert, who had the oars now. Tom made a big loop on the rope and threw it toward the house. But it only landed over a chicken, and caused the frightened fowl to fly high up in the air and rest in a tree on the bank.

"Good!" cried the people on the edge. "One is safe, anyhow!"

Tom threw the rope again. This time it caught on a corner of the henhouse, and as he pulled the knot tight they had the floating house secure.

"Hurrah, hurrah!" shouted the people.

By this time Mr. Mason and Uncle Daniel had reached the spot in their boat.

"Don't pull too hard!" called the men to the boys. "You'll upset your boat."

"Throw the line to us," added Uncle Daniel.

This the boys did, and as it was a long stretch of rope the men were able to get all the way in to shore with it before pulling at the house.

"Now we'll have a tug of war," said Mr. Mason.

"Wait for us!" cried the boys in the boat. "We want to have a pull at that."

All this time the chickens were cackling and screeching, as the house in the water lunged from one side to the other. It was a large new coop and built of strong material that made it very heavy.

"Now," said Uncle Daniel, as the boys reached the shore and secured their boat, "all take a good hold."

Every inch of the rope that crossed the water's edge was soon covered with somebody's hand.

"All pull now!" called Mr. Mason, and with a jerk in came the floating house, chickens, ducks, and all, and down went everybody that had pulled. The force of the jerk, of course, threw them all to the ground, but that was only fun and gave the boys a good chance to laugh.

Just as soon as the chickens reached the shore they scampered for home—some flying, some running, but all making a noise.

"We may as well finish the job," said Mr. Mason. "Tom, go hitch Sable up to the cart and we'll bring the henhouse back where it belongs."

By running across the fields that were on the

highest part of the road Tom was able to get to his barn without a boat, and soon he returned with the cart and Sable.

It took all hands to get the henhouse on the cart, but this was finally done, and away went Sable up the road with the queer load after him in the dump cart.

"You had better put it up on the hill this time," Peter told them. "The water isn't gone down yet." So at last the chicken coop was settled, and not a hen was missing.

There were many sights to be seen about Meadow Brook that afternoon, and the boys enjoyed the flood, now that there was no longer any danger to life.

Bert caught a big salmon and a black-spotted lizard that had been flooded out from some dark place in the mountains, Harry found a pretty toy canoe that some small boy had probably been playing with in the stream before the water rose, and Jack was kept busy towing in all kinds of stuff that had broken loose from barns along the pond.

Freddie had boots on, and was happy sailing his "ark" up and down the road. He insisted on Snoop taking a ride, but cats do not fancy water and the black kitten quickly hid himself up in the hay loft, out of Freddie's reach.

Little by little the water fell, until by the next

afternoon there was no longer a river running through the roads. But there were plenty of wet places and enough of streams washing down the road in the gutters to give Freddie a fine canal to sail boats in.

Nan and Flossie had boats too which Bert and Harry made for them. In fact, all the girls along Meadow Brook Road found something that would sail while the flood days lasted.

As it was still July the hot sun came down and dried things up pretty quickly, but many haymows were completely spoiled, as were summer vegetables that were too near the pond and came in for their share of the washout.

This loss, however, was nothing compared with what had been expected by the farmers, and all were satisfied that a kind Providence had saved the valley houses from complete destruction.

CHAPTER 18

THE FRESH-AIR CAMP

QUIET had settled down once more upon the little village of Meadow Brook. The excitement of the flood had died away, and now when the month of July was almost gone, and a good part of vacation had gone with it, the children turned their attention to a matter of new interest—the fresh-air camp.

"Mildred Manners was over to the camp yesterday," Nan told her mother, "and she says a whole lot of little girls have come out from the city, and they have such poor clothes. There is no sickness there that anyone could catch, she says (for her uncle is the doctor, you know), but Mildred says her mother is going to show her how to make some aprons for the little girls."

"Why, that would be nice for all you little girls to do," said Mrs. Bobbsey. "Suppose you start a sewing school, and all see what you can make?"

"Oh, that would be lovely!" exclaimed Nan.

"When can we start?"

"As soon as we get the materials," the mother replied. "We will ask Aunt Sarah to drive over to the camp this afternoon; then we can see what the children need."

"Can I go?" asked Flossie, much interested in the fresh-air work.

"I guess so," said Mrs. Bobbsey. "If we take the depot wagon there will be room for you and Freddie."

So that was how it came about that our little friends became interested in the fresh-air camp. Nan and Mildred, Flossie and Freddie, with Aunt Sarah and Mrs. Bobbsey, visited the camp in the afternoon.

"What a queer place it is!" whispered Flossie, as they drove up to the tents on the mountainside.

"Hush," said Nan. "They might hear you."

"Oh these are war camps!" exclaimed Freddie when he saw the white tents. "They're just like the war pictures in my storybook!"

The matron who had charge of the camp came up, and when Mrs. Bobbsey explained her business, the matron was pleased and glad to show them through the place.

"Oh, it was your boys who brought us all that money from the circus," said the woman. "That's why we have all the extra children here—the circus money has paid for them, and they are to have two weeks on this beautiful mountain."

"I'm glad the boys were able to help," said Mrs. Bobbsey. "It really was quite a circus."

"It must have been, when they made so much money," the other answered.

"And we are going to help now," spoke up Nan. "We are starting a sewing school."

"Oh, I'm so glad somebody has thought of clothes," said the matron. "We often get gifts of food, but we need clothes so badly."

"There is no sickness?" asked Mrs. Bobbsey, as they started on a tour of the camp.

"No, we cannot take sick children here now," said the matron. "We had some early in the season, but this is such a fine place for romping we decided to keep this camp for the healthy children and have another for those who are sick."

By this time numbers of little girls and boys crowded around the visitors. They were quite different from the children of Meadow Brook or Lakeport. Somehow they were smaller, but looked older. Poor children begin to worry so young that they soon look much older than they really are.

Nan and Mildred spoke kindly to the girls, while Freddie and Flossie soon made friends with the little boys. One small boy, smaller than Freddie, with sandy hair and beautiful blue eyes, was particularly happy with Freddie. He looked better than the others, was almost as fat as Freddie, and he had such lovely clear skin, as if somebody loved to wash it.

"Where do you lib?" he lisped to Freddie.

"At Uncle Daniel's," Freddie answered. "Where do you live?"

"With mamma," replied the little boy. Then he stopped a minute. "Oh, now, I don't live with mamma now," he corrected himself, "'cause she's gone to heaven, so I live with Mrs. Manily."

Mrs. Manily was the matron, and numbers of the children called her mamma.

"Can I come over and play with you?" asked the boy. "What's your name?"

"His name is Freddie and mine is Flossie," said the latter. "What is your name?"

"Mine is Edward Brooks," said the little stranger, "but everybody calls me Sandy. Do you like Sandy better than Edward?"

"No," replied Flossie. "But I suppose that's a pet name because your hair is that color."

"Is it?" said the boy, tossing his sunny curls around. "Maybe that's why!"

"Guess it is," said Freddie. "But will Mrs. Man let you come over to our house?"

"Mrs. Manily, you mean," said Sandy. "I'll just go and ask her."

"Isn't he cute!" exclaimed Flossie, and the pretty little boy ran in search of Mrs. Manily.

"I'm going to ask mamma if we can bring him home," declared Freddie. "He could sleep in my bed."

The others of the party were now walking through the big tents.

"This is where we eat," the matron explained, as the dining room was entered. The tent was filled with long narrow tables and had benches at the sides. The tables were covered with oilcloth, and in the center of each was a beautiful bunch of fresh wild flowers—the small pretty kind that grow in the woods.

"You ought to see our children eat," remarked the matron. "We have just as much as we can do to serve them, they have such good appetites from the country air."

"We must send you some fresh vegetables," said Aunt Sarah, "and some fruit for Sunday."

"We would be very grateful," replied Mrs. Manily, "for of course we cannot afford much of a variety."

Next to the dining room was the dormitory or sleeping tent.

"We have a little boys' brigade," said the matron, "and every pleasant evening they march around with drums and tin fifes. Then, when it is bedtime, we have a boy blow the 'taps' on a tin bugle, just like real soldiers do."

Freddie and Sandy had joined the sightseers now, and Freddie was much interested in the brigade.

"Who is the captain?" he asked of Mrs. Manily.

"Oh, we appoint a new captain each week from the very best boys we have. We only let a very good boy be captain," the matron told him.

In the dormitory were rows and rows of small white cots. They looked very clean and comfortable, and the door of this tent was closed with a big green mosquito netting.

"How old are your babies?" asked Aunt Sarah.

"Sandy is our baby!" replied the matron, patting the little boy fondly, "and he is four years old. We cannot take them any younger without their mothers."

"Freddie is four also," said Mrs. Bobbsey. "What a dear sweet child Sandy is!"

"Yes," said Mrs. Manily, "he has just lost a good mother and his father cannot care for him—that is, he cannot afford to pay his board or hire a housekeeper, so he brought him to the Aid Society. He is the pet of the camp, and you can see he has been brought up well."

"No mother and no home!" exclaimed Mrs. Bobbsey. "Dear little fellow! Think of our Freddie being alone in the world like that!"

Mrs. Bobbsey could hardly keep her tears back. She stooped over and kissed Sandy.

"Do you know my mamma?" he asked, looking straight into the lady's kind face.

"Mrs. Manily is your mamma, isn't she?" said Mrs. Bobbsey.

"Yes, she's my number two mamma, but I mean number one that used to sleep with me."

"Come now, Sandy," laughed Mrs. Manily. "Didn't you tell me last night I was the best mamma in the whole world?" and she hugged the little fellow to make him happy again.

"So you are," he laughed, forgetting all his loneliness now. "When I get to be a big man I'm goin' to take you out carriage riding."

"Can't Sandy come home with us?" asked Freddie. "He can sleep in my bed."

"You are very good," said the matron. "But we cannot let any of our children go visiting without special permission from the Society."

"Well," said Aunt Sarah, "if you get the permission we will be very glad to have Sandy pay us a visit. We have a large place, and would really like to have some good child enjoy it. We have company now, but they will leave us soon, and then perhaps we could have a little fresh-air camp of our own."

"The managers have asked us to look for a few

private homes that could accommodate some special cases," replied Mrs. Manily, "and I am sure I can arrange it to have Sandy go."

"Oh, let him come now," pleaded Freddie, as Sandy held tight to his hand. "See, we have room in the wagon."

"Well, he might have a ride," consented the matron, and before anyone had a chance to speak again Freddie and Sandy had climbed into the wagon.

Nan and Mildred had been talking to some of the older girls, who were very nice and polite for girls who had no one to teach them at home, and Nan declared that she was coming over to the camp to play with them some whole day.

"We can bring our lunch," said Mildred, "and you can show us all the pleasant play places you have fixed up in stones over the mountainside."

One girl, Nellie by name, seemed very smart and bright, and she brought to Mrs. Bobbsey a bunch of ferns and wild flowers she had just gathered while showing Nan and Mildred around.

"You certainly have a lovely place here," said Mrs. Bobbsey, as they got ready to leave, "and you little girls will be quite strong and ready for school again when you go back to the city."

"I don't go to school," said Nellie rather bashfully.

"Why?" asked Aunt Sarah.

"Oh, I go to night school," said the little girl. "But in the daytime I have to work."

"Why, how old are you?" asked Aunt Sarah.

"Twelve," said Nellie shyly.

"Working at twelve years of age!" exclaimed Mrs. Bobbsey in surprise. "What do you do?"

"I'm a cash-girl in a big store," said Nellie with some pride, for many little girls are not smart enough to hold such a position.

"I thought all children had to go to school," Aunt Sarah said to Mrs. Manily.

"So they do," replied the matron, "but in special cases they get permission from the factory inspector. Then they can work during the day and go to school at night."

"I think it's a shame!" said the mother. "That child is not much larger than Nan, and to think of her working in a big store all day, then having to work at night school too!"

"It does not seem right!" admitted the matron. "But, you see, sometimes there is no choice. Either a child must work or go to an institution, and we strain every point to keep them in their homes."

"We will drive back with Sandy," said Aunt Sarah as they got into the wagon.

"Can't Nellie come too?" asked Nan. "There is plenty of room."

The matron said yes, and so the little party started off for a ride along the pretty road.

"I was never in a carriage before in all my life," said Nellie suddenly. "Isn't it grand!"

"Never!" exclaimed the other girls in surprise.

"No," said Nellie. "I've had lots of rides in trolley cars, and we had a ride in a farm wagon the other day, but this is the first time I have ever been in a carriage."

Aunt Sarah was letting Sandy drive, and he, of course, was delighted. Freddie enjoyed it almost as well as Sandy did, and kept telling him which rein to pull on and all that. Old Bill, the horse, knew the road so well he really didn't need any driver, but he went along very nicely with the two little boys talking to him.

"We will stop and have some soda at the post office," said Mrs. Bobbsey. For the post office was also a general store.

This was good news to everybody, and when the man came out for the order Aunt Sarah told him to bring cakes too.

Everybody liked the ice cream soda, but it was plain Nellie and Sandy had not had such a treat in a long time.

"This is the best fun I've had!" declared the little cash-girl, showing how grateful she was. "And I hope you'll come and see us again," she added politely to Mildred and Nan.

"Oh, we intend to," said Mildred. "You know, we are going to have a sewing school to make aprons for the little ones at the camp."

Old Bill had turned back to the fresh-air quarters again, and soon, too soon, Sandy was handed back to Mrs. Manily, while Nellie jumped down and said what a lovely time she had had.

"Now be sure to come, Sandy," called Freddie, " 'cause I'll expect you!"

"I will," said Sandy rather sadly, for he would rather have gone along right then.

"And I'll let you play with Snoop and my playthings," Freddie called again. "Good-bye."

"Good-bye," answered the little fresh-air children.

Then old Bill took the others home.

CHAPTER 19

SEWING SCHOOL

"LET'S get Mabel and all the others," said Nan to Mildred. "We ought to take at least six gingham aprons and three nightgowns over to the camp."

Aunt Sarah had turned a big long attic room into a sewing school where Nan and Mildred had full charge. Flossie was to look after the spools of thread, keeping them from tangling up, and the girls agreed to let Freddie cut paper patterns.

This was not a play sewing school but a real one, for Aunt Sarah and Mrs. Bobbsey were to do the operating or machine sewing, while the girls were to sew on tapes, buttons, overhand seams, and do all that.

Mildred and Nan invited Mabel, Nettie, Marie Brenn (she was visiting the Herolds), Bessie, and Anna Thomas, a big girl who lived over Lakeside way.

"Be sure to bring your thimbles and needles," Nan told them. "And come at two o'clock this afternoon."

Every girl came—even Nettie, who was always so busy at home.

Mrs. Bobbsey sat at the machine ready to do stitching while Aunt Sarah was busy "cutting out" on a long table in front of the low window.

"Now, young ladies," said Mrs. Bobbsey, "we have ready some blue gingham aprons. You see how they are cut out; two seams, one at each side, then they are to be closed down the back. There will be a pair of strings on each apron, and you may begin by pressing down a narrow hem on these strings. We will not need to baste them, just press them down with the finger this way."

Mrs. Bobbsey then took up a pair of the sashes and turned in the edges. Immediately the girls followed her instructions, and very soon all of the strings were ready for the machine.

Nan handed them to her mother, and then Aunt Sarah gave out the work.

"Now these are the sleeves," said Aunt Sarah, "and they must each have little gathers brought in at the elbow here between these notches. Next you place the sleeve together notch to notch, and they can be stitched without basting."

"Isn't it lively to work this way?" said Mildred. "It isn't a bit of trouble, and see how quickly we get done."

"Many hands make light work," replied Mrs.

Bobbsey. "I guess we will get all the aprons finished this afternoon."

Piece by piece the various parts of the garments were given out, until there remained nothing more to do than to put on buttons and work buttonholes, and overband the armholes.

"I'll cut the buttonholes," said Mrs. Bobbsey, "then Nan and Mildred may work the buttonholes by sticking a pin through each hole. The other girls may then sew the buttons on."

It was wonderful how quickly those little pearl buttons went down the backs of the aprons.

"I believe I could make an apron all alone now," said Nan, "if it was cut out."

"So could I," declared Mildred. "It isn't hard at all."

"Well, here's my patterns," spoke up Freddie, who with Flossie had been busy over in the corner cutting "ladies" out of a fashion paper.

"No, they're paper dolls," said Flossie, who was standing them all up in a row, "and we are going to give them to the fresh-air children to play with on rainy days."

It was only half-past four when Nan rang the bell to dismiss the sewing school.

"We have had such a lovely time," said Mabel, "we would like to have sewing to do every week."

"Well, you are welcome to come," said Aunt

Sarah. "We will make night dresses for the poor little ones next week, then after that you might all bring your own work, mending, fancywork, or tidies, whatever you have to do."

"And we might each pay five cents to sew for the fresh-air children," suggested Mildred.

"Yes, all charity sewing classes have a fund," Mrs. Bobbsey remarked. "That would be a good idea."

"Now let us fold up the aprons," said Nan. "Don't they look pretty?"

And indeed the half-dozen blue and white ginghams did look very nice, for they were carefully made and all smooth and even.

"When can we iron them out?" asked Flossie, anxious to deliver the gifts to the needy little ones.

"Tomorrow afternoon," replied her mother. "The boys are going to pick vegetables in the morning, and we will drive over in the afternoon."

Uncle Daniel had given the boys permission to pick all the butter beans and string beans that were ripe, besides three dozen ears of the choicest corn, called "Country Gentleman."

"Children can only eat very tender corn," said Uncle Daniel, "and as that is sweet and milky they will have no trouble digesting it."

Harry looked over every ear of the green corn

by pulling the husks down and any that seemed a bit overripe he discarded.

"We will have to take the long wagon," said Bert, as they began to count up the baskets. There were two of beans, three of corn, one of lettuce, two of sweet apples, besides five bunches of Freddie's radishes.

"Be sure to bring Sandy back with you," called Freddie, who did not go to the camp this time. "Tell him I'll let him be my twin brother."

Nan and Aunt Sarah went with the boys, but how disappointed they were to find a strange matron in charge of the camp, and Sandy's eyes red from crying after Mrs. Manily.

"Oh, I knowed you would come to take me to Freddie," cried he, "'cause my other mamma is gone too, and I'm all alone."

"Mrs. Manily was called away by sickness in her family," explained the new matron, "and I cannot do anything with this little boy."

"He was so fond of Mrs. Manily," said Aunt Sarah, "and besides he remembers how lonely he was when his own mother went away. Maybe we could bring him over to our house for a few days."

"Yes, Mrs. Manily spoke of that," said the matron, "and she had received permission from the Society to let Edward pay a visit to Mrs. Daniel Bobbsey. See, here is the card."

"Oh, that will be lovely!" cried Nan, hugging Sandy as tight as her arms could squeeze. "Freddie told us to be sure to bring you back with us."

"I am so glad to get these things," the matron said to Aunt Sarah, as she took the aprons, "for everybody has been upset with Mrs. Manily having to leave so suddenly. The aprons are lovely. Did the little girls make them?"

Aunt Sarah told her about the sewing school, and then she said she was going to have a little account printed about it in the year's report of good work done for the Aid Society.

"And Mrs. Manily has written an account of your circus," the matron told Harry and Bert, for she had heard about the boys and their successful charity work.

Some of the girls who knew Nan came up now and told her how Nellie, the little cash-girl, had been taken sick and had had to be removed to the hospital tent over in the other mountain.

This was sad news to Nan, for she loved the little cash-girl, and hoped to see her and perhaps have her pay a visit to Aunt Sarah's.

"Is she very sick?" Aunt Sarah asked the matron.

"Yes indeed," the other replied. "But the doctor will soon cure her, I think."

"The child is too young to work so hard," Aunt

Sarah declared. "It is no wonder her health breaks down at the slightest cause, when she has no strength laid away to fight sickness."

By this time a big girl had washed and dressed Sandy, and now what a pretty boy he was! He wore a blue and white striped linen suit and had a jaunty little white cap just like Freddie's.

He was so anxious to go that he jumped in the wagon before the others were ready to start.

"Get app, Bill!" he called, grabbing at the reins, and off the old horse started with no one in the wagon but Sandy!

Sandy had given the reins such a jerk that Bill started to run, and the more the little boy tried to stop him the harder he went!

"Don't slap him with the reins!" called Harry, who was now running down the hill as hard as he could after the wagon. "Pull on the reins!" he called again.

But Sandy was so excited he kept slapping the straps up and down on poor Bill, which to the horse, of course, meant to go faster.

"He'll drive in the brook," called Bert in alarm, also rushing after the runaway.

"Whoa, Bill! Whoa, Bill!" called everybody, the children from the camp having now joined in following the wagon.

The brook was directly in front of Sandy.

"Quick, Harry!" yelled Bert. "You'll get him in a minute."

It was no easy matter, however, to overtake Sandy, for the horse had been on a run from the start. But Sandy kept his seat well, and even seemed to think it good fun now to have everybody running after him and no one able to catch him.

"Oh, I'm so afraid he'll go in the pond!" Nan told Aunt Sarah almost in tears.

"Bill would sit down first," declared Aunt Sarah, who knew her horse to be an intelligent animal.

"Oh, oh, oh!" screamed everybody, for the horse had crossed from the road into the little field that lay next to the water.

"Whoa, Bill!" shouted Aunt Sarah at the top of her voice, and instantly the horse stood still.

The next minute both Bert and Harry were in the wagon beside Sandy.

"Can't I drive?" asked the little fellow innocently, while Harry was backing out of the swamp.

"You certainly made Bill go," Harry admitted, all out of breath from running.

"And you gave us a good run, too," added Bert, who was red in the face from his violent exercise.

"Bill knew ma meant it when she said whoa!" Harry remarked to Bert. "I tell you, he stopped just in time, for a few feet further would have sunk horse, wagon, and all in the swamp."

Of course it was all an accident, for Sandy had no idea of starting the horse off, so no one blamed him when they got back to the road.

"We'll all get in this time," laughed Aunt Sarah to the matron. "And I'll send the boys over Sunday to let you know how Sandy is."

"Oh, he will be all right with Freddie!" Bert said, patting the little stranger on the shoulder. "We will take good care of him."

It was a pleasant ride back to the Bobbsey farm, and all enjoyed it—especially Sandy, who had gotten the idea he was a first-class driver and knew all about horses, old Bill, in particular.

"Hurrah, hurrah!" shouted Freddie, when the wagon turned in the drive. "I knowed you would come, Sandy!" and the next minute the two little boys were hand in hand running up to the barn to see Frisky, Snoop, the chickens, ducks, pigeons, and everything at once.

Sandy was a little city boy and knew nothing about real live country life, so that everything seemed quite wonderful to him, especially the chickens and ducks. He was rather afraid of anything as big as Frisky.

Snoop and Fluffy were put through their circus tricks for the stranger's benefit, and then Freddie let Sandy turn on his trapeze up under the apple tree and showed him all the different kinds of turns Bert and Harry had taught the younger twin how to perform on the swing.

"How long can you stay?" Freddie asked his little friend, while they were swinging.

"I don't know," Sandy replied vaguely.

"Maybe you could go to the seashore with us," Freddie ventured. "We are only going to stay in the country this month."

"Maybe I could go," lisped Sandy, " 'cause nobody ain't got charge of me now. Mrs. Manily has gone away, you know, and I don't b'lieve in the other lady, do you?"

Freddie did not quite understand this, but he said "no" just to agree with Sandy.

"And you know the big girl, Nellie, who always combed my hair without pulling it, she's gone away too, so maybe I'm your brother now," went on the little orphan.

"Course you are!" spoke up Freddie manfully, throwing his arms around the other, "You're my twin brother, too, 'cause that's the realest kind. We are all twins, you know—Nan and Bert, and Flossie and me and you!"

By this time the other Bobbseys had come out to welcome Sandy. They thought it best to let Freddie entertain him at first, so that he would not be strange, but now Uncle Daniel just took the little fellow up in his arms and into his heart, for all good men love boys, especially when they're such real little men as Sandy and Freddie happened to be.

"He's my twin brother, Uncle Daniel," Freddie insisted. "Don't you think he's just like me—curls and all?"

"He is certainly a fine little chap!" the uncle replied, meaning every word of it, "and he is quite some like you too. Now let us feed the chickens. See how they are around us expecting something to eat!"

The fowls were almost ready to eat the pearl buttons off Sandy's coat, so eager were they for their meal, and it was great fun for the two little boys to toss the corn to them.

"Granny will eat from your hand," exclaimed Uncle Daniel. "You see, she is just like granite-grey stone, but we call her Granny for short."

The Plymouth Rock hen came up to Sandy, and much to his delight ate the corn out of his little white hand.

"Oh, she's a pretty chicken!" he said, stroking Granny as he would a kitten. "I dust love chitens," he added, sitting right down on the sandy ground to let Granny come up on his lap. There was so much to see in the poultry yard that Sandy, Freddie, and Uncle Daniel lingered there until Martha appeared at the back door and rang the big dinner bell in a way that meant, "Hurry up! Something will get cold if you don't."

And the something proved to be chicken pot-pie with dumplings that everybody loves. And after that there came apple pudding with hard sauce, just full of sugar.

"Is it a party?" Sandy whispered to Freddie, for he was not accustomed to more than bread and milk at his evening meal.

"Yes, I guess so," ventured Freddie. "It's because you came," and then Dinah brought in little play cups of chocolate with jumbles on the side, and Mrs. Bobbsey said that would be better than the pudding for Freddie and Sandy.

"I guess I'll just live here," solemnly said the little stranger, as if his decision in such a matter should not be questioned.

"I guess you better!" Freddie agreed, "'cause it's nicer than over there, isn't it?"

"Lots," replied Sandy, "only maybe Mrs. Manily will cry for me," and he looked sad as his big blue eyes turned around and blinked to keep back some tears. "I dust love Mrs. Manily, Freddie. Don't you?" he asked wistfully.

Then Harry and Bert jumped up to start the phonograph, and that was like a bandwagon to the little fellows, who liked to hear the popular tunes called off by the funny man in the big bright horn.

CHAPTER 20

A MIDNIGHT SCARE

"Sometimes I'm afraid in the bed tent over there," said Sandy to Freddie. "'Cause there ain't nothing to keep the dark out but a piece of veil in the door."

"Mosquito netting," corrected Freddie. "I would be afraid to sleep outdoors that way too. 'Cause maybe there's snakes."

"There sure is," declared the other little fellow, cuddling up closer to Freddie. "'Cause one of the boys, Tommy his name, killed two the other day."

"Well, there ain't no snakes around here," declared Freddie, "an' this bed was put in this room, right next to mamma's, for me, so you needn't be scared when Aunt Sarah comes and turns out the lights."

Both little boys were very sleepy, and in spite of having so many things to tell each other the sandman came around and interrupted them, actually making their eyes fall down like porch screens when someone touches the string.

Mrs. Bobbsey came up and looked in at the door.

Two little sunny heads so close together!

"Why should that little darling be left alone over in the dark tent!" she thought. "See how happy he is with our own dear son Freddie."

Then she tucked them a little bit, half closed the door, and turned out the hall light.

Everybody must have been dreaming for hours, it seemed so at any rate, when suddenly all were awake again.

What was it?

What woke up the household with such a start?

"There it is again!" screamed Flossie. "Oh, mamma, mamma, come in my room quick!"

Sandy grabbed hold of Freddie.

"We're all right," whispered the brave little Freddie. "It's only the girls that's hollering."

Then they both put their curls under the bed quilts.

"Someone's playing the piano," Bert said to Harry, and sure enough, a nocturnal solo was coming up in queer chunks from the parlor.

"It's a crazy burglar, and he never saw a piano before," Flossie said.

The hall clock just struck midnight. That

seemed to make everybody more frightened.

Uncle Daniel was hurrying down the stairs now.

"There it is again," whispered Bert, as another group of wild chords came from the piano.

"It must be cats!" exclaimed Uncle Daniel. "Harry, come down here and help light up, and we'll solve this mystery."

Without a moment's hesitation Bert and Harry were down the stairs and had the hall light burning as quickly as a good match could be struck.

"Where is Snoop?" asked Uncle Daniel.

The boys opened the hall door into the cellar-way, and found there Snoop on his cushion and Fluffy on hers.

"It wasn't the cats," they declared.

"What could it be?"

Uncle Daniel even lighted the piano lamp, which gave a strong light, but there didn't seem to be any disturbance about.

"It certainly was the piano," he said, much puzzled.

"And sounded like a cat serenade," ventured Harry.

"Well, she isn't around here," laughed Uncle Daniel, "and we never heard of a ghost in Meadow Brook before."

All this time the people upstairs waited anxiously. Flossie held Nan so tightly about the neck that the elder sister could hardly breathe, Freddie and Sandy were still under the bedclothes, while Mrs. Bobbsey and Aunt Sarah listened in the hall.

"That sure is a ghost," whispered Dinah to Martha in the hall above. "Ghosts always love music."

"Ghosts nothin'," replied Martha indignantly. "I dusted every key of the piano today, and I guess I could smell a ghost about as quickly as anybody."

"Well, I don't see that we can do any good by sitting around here," remarked Uncle Dan to the boys, after the lapse of some minutes. "We may as well put out the lights and get into bed again."

"But I cannot see what it could be!" Mrs. Bobbsey insisted, as they all prepared to retire again.

"Neither can we!" agreed Uncle Daniel. "Maybe our piano has one of those self-playing tricks, and somebody wound it up by accident."

But no sooner were the lights out and the house quiet than the piano started again.

"Hush! Keep quiet!" whispered Uncle Daniel. "I'll get it this time, whatever it is!"

With matches in one hand and a candle in the other he started downstairs in the dark without making a sound, while the piano kept on playing in "chunks" as Harry said, same as it did before.

Once in the parlor Uncle Daniel struck a match and put it to the candle, and then the music ceased.

"There he is," he called, and Flossie thought she surely would die.

Slam! went the music book at something, and Sandy almost choked with fear.

Bang! went something else, that brought Bert and Harry downstairs to help catch the burglar.

"There he is in the corner!" called Uncle Daniel to the boys, and then began such a slam-banging time that the people upstairs were in terror that the burglar would kill Harry and Bert and Uncle Daniel.

"We've got him! We've got him!" declared Harry, while Bert lighted the lamp.

"Is he dead?" screamed Aunt Sarah from the stairs.

"As a doornail!" answered Harry.

"What is it?" asked Mrs. Bobbsey, hardly able to speak.

"A big grey rat," replied Uncle Daniel, and everybody had a good laugh.

"I thought it might be that," said Mrs. Bobbsey.

"So did I," declared Nan. "But I wasn't sure."

"I thought it was a big burglar," Flossie said,

her voice still shaking from the fright.

"I thought it was a policeman," faltered Sandy. "'Cause they always bang things like that."

"And I thought, sure as your life, it was a real ghost," laughed Dinah. "'Cause the clock just struck for the ghost hour."

"He must have come in from the fields where John has been plowing. Like a cat in a strange garret, he didn't know what to do in a parlor," said Uncle Daniel.

Harry took the candle and looked carefully over the keys.

"Why, there's something like seeds on the keys!"

"Oh, I have it!" exclaimed Bert. "Nan left her hat on the piano last night, and it has those funny straw flowers on it. See, the rat got some of them off and they dropped on the keys."

"And the other time he came for the cake," said Aunt Sarah.

"That's it," declared Uncle Daniel, "and each time we scared him off he came back again to finish his meal. But I guess he is through now," and so saying he took the dead rodent and raising the side window tossed him out.

It was some time before everybody got quieted down again, but finally the rat scare was over and the Bobbseys turned to dreams of the happy summertime they were enjoying.

When Uncle Dan came up from the post office the next morning he brought a note from the fresh-air camp.

"Sandy has to go back!" Nan whispered to Bert. "His own father in the city has sent for him, but mamma says not to say anything to Sandy or Freddie—they might worry. Aunt Sarah will drive over and bring Sandy, then they can fix it. I'm so sorry he has to go away."

"So am I," answered Nan's twin. "I don't see why they can't let the little fellow alone when he is happy with us."

"But it's his own father, you know, and something about a rich aunt. Maybe she is going to adopt Sandy."

"We ought to adopt him; he's all right with us," Bert grumbled. "What did his rich aunt let him cry his eyes out for if she cared anything for him?"

"Maybe she didn't know about him, then," Nan considered. "I'm sure everybody would have to love Sandy."

At that Sandy ran along the path with Freddie. He looked like a live buttercup, so fresh and bright, his sunny sandy curls blowing in the soft breeze. Mrs. Bobbsey had just called the children to her.

"We are going over to see Mrs. Manily today, Sandy," she said. "Won't you be awfully glad to see your own dear Mamma Manily again?"

"Yep," he faltered, getting a better hold on Freddie's hand, "but I want to come back here," he finished.

Poor darling! So many changes of home in his life had made him fear another.

"Oh, I am sure you will come to see us again," Mrs. Bobbsey declared. "Maybe you can come to Lakeport when we go home in the fall."

"No, I'm comin' back here," he insisted, "to see Freddie, and auntie, and uncle, and all of them."

"Well, we must get ready now," said Mrs. Bobbsey. "John has gone to bring the wagon."

Freddie insisted upon going to the camp with Sandy, "to make sure he would come down again," he said.

It was only the happiness of seeing Mamma Manily once more that kept Sandy from crying when they told him he was to go on a great big fast train to see his own papa.

"You see," Mrs. Manily explained to Mrs. Bobbsey, "a wealthy aunt of Edward's expects to adopt him, so we will have to give him up, I am afraid."

"I hope you can keep track of him," answered

Mrs. Bobbsey, "for we are all so attached to him. I think we would have applied to the Aid Society to let him share our home if the other claim had not come first and taken him from us."

Then Freddie kissed Sandy good-bye. It was not the kind of a caress that girls give, but the two little fellows said good-bye, kissed each other very quickly, then looked down at the ground in a brave effort not to cry.

Mrs. Bobbsey gave Sandy a real mother's love kiss, and he said:

"Oh, I'm comin' back—tomorrow. I won't stay in the city. I'll just run away and come back."

So Sandy was gone to another home, and we hope he will grow to be as fine a boy as he has been a loving child.

"How lonely it seems," said Nan that afternoon. "Sandy was so jolly."

Freddie followed John all over the place, and could not find anything worth doing. Even Dinah sniffed a little when she fed the kittens and didn't have "that little buttercup around to tease him."

"Well," said Uncle Daniel next day, "we are going to have a very poor crop of apples this year, so I think we had better have some cider made from the early fruit. Harry and Bert, you can help John if you like, and take a load of apples to the cider mill today to be ground."

The boys willingly agreed to help John, for they liked that sort of work, especially Bert, to whom it was new.

"We'll take the red astrachans and sheep-noses today," John said. "Those trees over there are loaded, you see. Then there are the orange apples in the next row; they make good cider."

The early apples were very plentiful, and it took scarcely any time to make up a load and start off for the cider mill.

"Old Bennett who runs the mill is a queer chap," Harry told Bert going over. "He's a soldier, and he'll be sure to quiz you on history."

"I like old soldiers," Bert declared. "If they do talk a lot, they've got a lot to talk about."

John said that was true, and he agreed that old Ben Bennett was an interesting talker.

"Here we are," said Harry, as they pulled up before a kind of barn. Old Ben sat outside on his wooden bench.

"Hello, Ben," they called out together. "We're bringing you work early this year."

"So much the better," said the old soldier. "There's nothing like work to keep a fellow young."

"Well, you see," went on John, "we can't count on any late apples this year, so, as we must have cider, we thought that we had better make hay while the sun shines."

186

"How much have you got there?" asked Ben, looking over the load.

"About a barrel, I guess," answered John. "Could you run them through for us this morning?"

"Certainly, certainly!" replied the other. "Just haul them on, and we'll set to work as quick as we did that morning at Harper's Ferry. Who is this lad?" he asked, indicating Bert.

"My cousin from the city," said Harry. "Bert's his name."

"Glad to see you, Bert, glad to see you!" and the old soldier shook hands warmly. "When they call you out, son, just tell them you knew Ben Bennett of the Sixth Massachusetts. And they'll give you a good gun," and he clapped Bert on the back as if he actually saw a war coming down the hill back of the cider mill.

It did not take long to unload the apples and get them inside.

"We'll feed them in the hopper," said John, "if you just get the sacks out, Ben."

"All right, all right, my lad; you can fire the first volley if you've a mind to," and Ben opened up the big cask that held the apples to be chopped. When a few bushels had been filled in by the boys John began to grind. He turned the big stick round and round, and this in turn set the wheel in motion that held the knives that chopped the apples.

"Where does the cider come from?" asked Bert, much interested.

"We haven't come to that yet," Harry replied. "They have to go through this hopper first."

"Fine juicy apples," remarked Ben. "Don't know but it's just as well to make cider now when you have a crop like this."

"Father thought so," Harry added, putting in the last scoop of sheep-noses. "If it turns to vinegar we can use it for pickles this fall."

The next part of the process seemed very queer to Bert; the pulp or chopped apples were put in sacks like meal bags, folded over so as to hold in the pulp. A number of the folded sacks were then placed in another machine "like a big layer cake," Bert said, and by turning a screw a great press was brought down upon the soft apples.

"Now the boys can turn," John suggested, and at this both Bert and Harry grabbed hold of the long handle that turned the press and started on a run around the machine.

"Oh, there she comes!" cried Bert, as the juice began to ooze out in the tub. "That's cider all right! I smell it."

"Fine and sweet too," declared Ben, seeing to

it that the tub was well under the spout. "But I don't want you young fellows to do all my work."

"Oh, this is fun," spoke up Bert, as the color mounted to his cheeks from the exercise. A strong stream was pouring into the tub now, and the wholesome odor of good sweet cider filled the room.

"I think I'll try to get a horse this fall when my next pension comes due," said old Ben. "I'm a little too stiff to run around with that handle like you young lads, and sometimes I'm full of rheumatism too."

"Father said he would sell our Bill very cheap if he wasn't put at hard work," Harry said. "We have had him so long we don't want to see him put to a plow or anything heavy, but I should think this would be quite easy for him."

"Just the thing for a worn-out warhorse like myself," answered Ben, much interested. "Tell your father not to think of selling Bill till I get a chance to see him. I won't have my pension money for two months yet, but I might make a deposit if any more work comes in."

"Oh, that would be all right," spoke up John. "Mr. Bobbsey would not be afraid to trust you."

"There now!" exclaimed Ben. "I guess you've got all the juice out. John, you can fill it in your keg, I suppose, since you have been so good as to do all the rest. Will you try it, boys?"

"Yes, we would like to, Ben," Harry replied. "It's a little warm to make cider in July," and he wiped his face to cool off some.

Ben went to his homemade cupboard and brought out a tin cup.

"There's a cup," he said, "that I drank out of at Harper's Ferry. I keep it in everyday use, so as not to lose sight of it."

Bert took the old tin cup and regarded it reverently.

"Think of us drinking out of that cup," reflected Bert. "Why, it's a war relic!"

"How's the cider?" asked the old soldier.

"Couldn't be better," said Harry. "I guess the cup helps the flavor."

This pleased old Ben, for the light of glory that comes to all veterans, whether private or general, shone in his eyes.

"Well, a soldier has two lives," he declared. "The one under fire and the other here," tapping his head and meaning that the memories of battles made the other life.

The cider was ready now, and the Bobbseys prepared to leave.

"I'll tell father about Bill," said Harry. "I'm sure he will save him for you."

"All right, sonny—thank you, thank you! Good-bye, lads; come again, and maybe some day I'll give you the war cup!" called the soldier.

"That would be a relic!" exclaimed Harry. "And I guess father will give him Bill for nothing, for we always do what we can for old soldiers."

"I never saw cider made before," remarked Bert, "and I think it's fun. I had a good time today."

"Glad you did," said John, "for vacation is slipping now and you want to enjoy it while it lasts."

That evening at dinner the new cider was sampled, and everybody pronounced it very fine.

CHAPTER 21

WHAT THE WELL CONTAINED

THE next day everybody was out early.

"The men are going to clean the well," Harry told the others, "and it's lots of fun to see all the stuff they bring up."

"Can we go?" Freddie asked.

"Nan will have to take charge of you and Flossie," said Mrs. Bobbsey, "for wells are very dangerous, you know."

This was arranged, and the little ones promised to do exactly as Nan told them.

The well to be cleaned was the big one at the corner of the road and the lane. From the well a number of families got their supply of water, and it being on the road many passersby also enjoyed from it a good cold drink.

"There they come," called Bert, as two men dressed like divers came up the road.

They wore complete rubber suits, hip boots, rubber coats, and rubber caps. Then they had some queer-looking machines, a windlass, a force pump, grappling irons, and other tools.

The boys gathered around the men—all interested, of course in the work.

"Now keep back," ordered Nan to the little ones. "You can see just as well from this big stone, and you will not be in any danger here."

So Freddie and Flossie mounted the rock while the large boys got in closer to the well.

First the men removed the well shelter—the wooden house that covered the well. Then they put over the big hole a platform open in the center. Over this they set up the windlass, and then one of the men got in a big bucket.

"Oh, he'll get drownded!" cried Freddie.

"No, he won't," said Flossie. "He's a diver like's in my picture book."

"Is he, Nan?" asked the other little one.

"Yes, he is one kind of a diver," the sister explained, "only he doesn't have to wear that funny hat with air pipes in it like ocean divers wear."

"But he's away down in the water now," persisted Freddie. "Maybe he's dead."

"See, there he is up again," said Nan, as the man in the bucket stepped out on the platform over the well.

"He just went down to see how deep the water

was," Bert called over. "Now they are going to pump it out."

The queer-looking pump, with great long pipes, was now sunk into the well, and soon a strong stream of water was flowing from the spout.

"Oh, let's sail boats!" exclaimed Freddie, and then all the bits of clean sticks and boards around were turned into boats by Flossie and Freddie. As the water had a good clear sweep down the hill the boats went along splendidly, and the little folks had a very fine time of it indeed.

"Don't fall in," called Nan. "Freddie, look out for that deep hole in the gutter, where the tree fell down in the big flood."

But for once Freddie managed to save himself, while Flossie took no risk at all, but walked past that part of the "river" without guiding her "steamboat."

Presently the water in the "river" became weaker and weaker, until only the smallest stream made its way along.

"We can't sail boats in mud," declared Freddie with some impatience. "Let's go back and see what they're doing at the well."

Now the big pump had been removed and the man was going down in the bucket again.

"We lost lots of things in there," remarked Tom Mason. "I bet they'll bring up some queer stuff."

It took a few minutes for the other man to send the lanterns down after his companion and then remove the top platform so as to give all the air and light possible to the bottom of the well.

"Now the man in the well can see stars in the sky," said Harry to the other boys.

"But there are no stars in the sky," Bert contradicted, looking up at the clear blue sky of the fine summer day.

"Oh, yes there are!" laughed the man at the well. "Lots of them too, but you can only see them in the dark, and it's good and dark down in that deep well."

This seemed very strange, but of course it was true; and the well cleaner told them if they didn't believe it, just to look up a chimney some day, and they would see the same strange thing.

At a signal from the man in the well the other raised the first bucket of stuff and dumped it on the ground.

"Hurrah! Our football!" exclaimed Harry, yanking out from the muddy things the big black rubber ball lost the year before.

"And our baseball," called Tom Mason, as another ball was extracted from the pile.

"Peter Burns' dinner pail," laughed Harry, rescuing that article from the heap.

"And somebody's old shoe!" put in Bert, but

he didn't bother pulling that out of the mud.

"Oh, there's Nellie Prentice's rubber doll!" exclaimed Harry. "August and Ned were playing ball with it and let it fly in the well."

Harry wiped the mud off the doll and brought it over to Nan.

"I'm sure Nellie will be glad to get this back," said Nan, "for it's a good doll, and she probably never had one since she lost it."

The doll was not injured by its long imprisonment in the well and when washed up was as good as ever. Nan took charge of it, and promised to give it to Nellie just as soon as she could go over to see her.

Another bucket of stuff had been brought up by that time, and the first thing pulled out was a big long pipe, the kind Germans generally use.

"That's old Hans Bruen's," declared Tom. "I remember the night he dropped it."

"Foolish Hans—to try to drink with a pipe like that in his mouth!" laughed the well cleaner.

As the pipe had a wooden bowl and a hard porcelain stem it was not broken, so Tom took care of it, knowing how glad Hans would be to get his old friend "Johnnie Smoker" back again.

Besides all kinds of tin cups, pails, and saucepans, the well was found to contain a good number of boys' caps and some girls' too, that had slipped off in attempts made to get a good cool drink out of the bucket.

Finally the man gave a signal that he was ready to come up, and soon the windlass was adjusted again and the man in very muddy boots came to the top.

"Look at this!" he said to the boys, holding a beautiful gold watch. "Ever hear of anyone losing a watch in the well?"

No one had heard of such a loss, and as there was no name anywhere on the watch that might lead to its identification, the well cleaner put it away in his vest pocket under the rubber coat.

"And what do you think of this?" the man continued, and drew from his pocket a beautiful string of pearl beads set in gold.

"My beads! My lost beads!" screamed Nan. "Oh, how glad I am that you found them!"

She took the beads and looked at them carefully. They were a bit dirty, but otherwise as good as ever.

"I thought I should never see them again," said Nan. "I must tell mamma of this!" And she started for the house with flying feet. Mrs. Bobbsey was glad indeed to learn that the string of pearls had been found, and everybody declared that Nan was certainly lucky.

"I am going to fasten them on good and tight

after this," said Nan, and she did.

Down by the well the man was not yet through handing over the things he had found.

"And there's a wedding ring!" he said next, while he turned out in his hand a thin gold band.

"Oh, Mrs. Burns lost that!" chorused a number of the boys. "She felt dreadful over it too. She'll be tickled to get that back all right."

"Well, here," said the man, turning to Harry. "I guess you're the biggest boy; I'll let you take that back to Mrs. Burns with my best wishes," and he handed Harry the long-lost wedding ring.

It was only a short distance to Mrs. Burns' house, and Harry lost no time in getting there.

"She was just delighted," Harry told the man, upon returning to the well. "She says Peter will send you over something for finding it."

"No need," replied the other. "They're welcome to their own."

The last part of the well-cleaning was the actual scrubbing of the big stone in the bottom. This stone had a hole in the middle through which the water sprang up, and when the flag had been scrubbed the well was clean indeed.

"Now you people will have good water," declared the men, as they gathered all their tools, having first put the top on the well and tried a bucketful of water before starting off.

"And are there really stars in the bottom of the well?" questioned Freddie.

"Not exactly," said the man, "but there are lots of other things in the bottoms of wells. You must get your daddy to show you the sky through a fire-place, and you will then know how the stars look in daylight," he finished, saying good-bye to all and starting off for the big deep well pump over in the picnic grove, that had not been cleaned since it had been dug there three years before.

CHAPTER 22

LITTLE JACK HORNER—GOOD-BYE

"I'VE got a special delivery letter for you," called the boy from the post office to Harry.

Now when Jim Dexter rode his wheel with the special delivery mail everybody about Meadow Brook knew the rush letter bore important news.

Jim jumped off his wheel and, opening the little bag, pulled out a letter for Mrs. Richard Bobbsey from Mrs. William Minturn of Ocean Cliff.

"I'll take it upstairs and have your book signed," Harry offered, while Jim sat on the porch to rest.

"That's from Aunt Emily," Bert told Harry when the messenger boy rode off again. "I guess we're going down to Ocean Cliff to visit there."

"I hope you won't go very soon," replied Harry. "We've arranged a lot of ball matches next month. We're going to play the school nine first, then we're to play the boys at Cedarhurst and a picked nine from South Meadow Brook."

"I'd like first-rate to be here for the games," said Bert. "I'm a good batter."

"You're the player we need then, for Jim Smith is a first-rate pitcher and we've got really a fine catcher in Tom Mason, but it's hard to get a fellow to hit the ball far enough to give us runs."

"Oh, Bert!" called Nan, running out of the house. "That was an invitation for us to go to Aunt Emily's at the seashore. And Cousin Dorothy says we will have such a lovely time! But I'm sure we could never have a better time than we had here, Harry," she added to her cousin.

"I'll be awfully sorry to have you go, Nan," replied Harry. "We have had so much fun all month. I'll just be dead lonesome, I'm sure," and Harry sat down in dejection, just as if his loved cousins had gone already.

"There's no boy at Uncle William's," said Bert. "Of course Nan will have Dorothy, but I'll have to look around for a chum, I suppose."

"Oh, you'll find lots of boys at the beach," said Harry. "And to think of the fun at the ocean! Mother says we will go to the shore next summer."

"I wish you were going with us," said Bert politely.

"Maybe you will come down for a day while we are there," suggested Nan. "Aunt Emily isn't just exactly your aunt, because she's mamma's sister, and it's papa who is Uncle Daniel's brother. But the Minturns, Aunt Emily's folks, you know, have been up here and are all like real cousins."

"We're going away!" exclaimed Freddie, joining the others just then. "Mamma says I can stick my toes in the water till the crabs bite me, but I'm going to have a fishhook and catch them first."

"Are you going to take Snoop?" Harry asked his little cousin.

"Yep," replied the youngster. "He knows how to go on trains now."

"Dorothy has a pair of donkeys," Nan told them, "and a cart we can go riding in every day."

"I'll be the driver," announced Freddie.

"And I suppose you'll have a sailboat, Bert!" said Harry.

"Not in the ocean," said nervous little Flossie, who had been listening all the time and never said a word until she thought there was some danger coming.

"Certainly not," said Bert. "There is always a little lake of quiet water around ocean places."

Aunt Sarah came out now, all dressed for a drive.

"Well, my dears," she said, "you are going to Ocean Cliff tomorrow, so you can invite all your Meadow Brook friends to a little lawn party today.

I'm going down now to the village to order some good things for you. I want you all to have a nice time this afternoon."

"I'm going to give some of my books to Nettie," said Flossie, "and some of my paper dolls too."

"Yes. Nettie has not many things to play with," agreed Nan, "and we can get plenty more."

"I'm going to get all my birds' nests together," said Bert, "and that pretty white birch bark to make picture frames for Christmas."

"I've got lovely pressed flowers to put on Christmas postcards," said Nan. "I'm going to mount them on plain white cards with little verses written for each friend. Won't that be pretty?"

Then what a time there was packing up again! Of course Mrs. Bobbsey had expected to go, and had most of the big things ready, but the children had so many souvenirs.

"John gave me this," cried Freddie, pulling a great big pumpkin in his express wagon down to the house. "And I'm going to bring it to Aunt Emily."

"Oh, how could we bring that!" protested Nan.

"In the trunk, of course," Freddie insisted.

"Well, I have to carry a box of ferns," said Flossie. "I'm going to take them for the porch. There are ferns around the salt water, mamma says."

So each child had his or her own pet remembrances to carry away from Meadow Brook.

"We had better go and invite the girls for the afternoon," Nan said to Flossie.

"And we must look after the boys," Harry told Bert.

A short invitation was not considered unusual in the country, so it was an easy matter to get all the children together in time for the farewell lawn party.

"We all hope you will come again next year," said Mildred Manners. "We have had such a lovely time this summer. And I brought you this little handkerchief to remember me by."

The gift was a choice bit of lace, and Nan was much pleased to accept it.

"There is something to remember me by," said Mabel Herold, presenting Nan with a postcard album.

The little girls brought Flossie a gold-striped cup and saucer, a set of doll's patterns, and the dearest little parasol. This last was from Bessie Dimple.

And Nettie brought—what do you think?

A little live duck for Freddie!

It was just like a lump of cotton batting, so soft and fluffy.

"We'll fatten him up for Christmas," laughed Bert, joking.

"No, you won't!" snapped Freddie. "I am going

to have a little house for him and a lake, and a boat—"

"Are you going to teach him to row?" teased Harry.

"Well, he can swim better than—than—"

"August Stout," answered Bert, remembering how August had fallen in the pond the day they went fishing.

When the ice cream and cake had been served on the lawn, Mrs. Bobbsey brought out a big round white paper pie. This she placed in the middle of a nice clean spot on the lawn, and all around the pie she drew out long white ribbons. On each ribbon was pinned the name of one of the guests.

"Now this is your Jack Horner pie," said Mrs. Bobbsey, "and when you put in your thumb you will pull out a plum."

Nan read off the names, and each girl or boy took the place assigned. Finally everybody had in hand a ribbon.

"Nettie has number one," said Nan. "You pull first, Nettie."

Nettie jerked her ribbon and pulled out on the end of it the dearest little play piano. It was made of paper, of course, and so very small it could stand on Nettie's hand.

"Give us a tune!" laughed the boys, while

Nettie saw it really was a little box of candy.

"Mildred next," announced Nan.

On the end of Mildred's ribbon came an automobile!

This caused a laugh, for Mildred was very fond of automobile rides.

Mabel got a hobbyhorse—because she was learning to ride horseback.

Nan received a sewing machine, to remind her of the fresh-air work.

Of course Tom Mason got a horse—a donkey it really was; and Jack Hopkins' gift was a wheelbarrow. Harry pulled out a boat, and Bert got a cider barrel.

They were all souvenirs, full of candy, favors for the party, and they caused no end of fun.

Freddie was the last to pull and he got—

A bunch of real radishes from his own garden!

"But they're not candy," he protested, as he burned his tongue with one.

"Well, we are going to let you and Flossie put your thumbs in the pie," said his mamma, "and whoever gets the prize will be the real Jack Horner."

All but the center of the pie was gone now, and in this Flossie first put her thumb. She could only put in one finger and only fish just one, and she brought out—a little gold ring from Aunt Sarah.

"Oh, isn't it sweet!" the girls all exclaimed.

Then Freddie had his turn.

"Can't I put in two fingers?" he pleaded.

"No, only one!" his mother insisted.

After careful preparation Freddie put in his thumb and pulled out a big candy plum!

"Open it!" called Nan.

The plum was put together in halves, and when Freddie opened it he found a real "going" watch from Uncle Daniel.

"I can tell time!" declared the happy boy, for he had been learning the hours on Martha's clock in the kitchen.

"What time is it, then?" asked Bert.

Freddie looked at his watch and counted around it two or three times.

"Four o'clock!" he said at last, and he was only twenty minutes out of the way. The watch was the kind little boys use first, with very plain figures on it, and it was quite certain before Freddie paid his next visit to Uncle Daniel's he would have learned how to tell time exactly on his first "real" watch.

The party was over, the children said good-bye, and besides the play favors each carried away a real gift, that of friendship for the little Bobbseys.

"Maybe you can come down to the seashore on an excursion," said Nan to her friends. "They often have Sunday school excursions to Sunset Beach."

"We will if we can," answered Mabel, "but if I don't see you there, I may call on you at Lakeport, when we go to the city."

"Oh yes, do!" insisted Nan. "I'll be home all winter I guess, but I might go to boarding school. Anyhow, I'll write to you. Good-bye, girls!"

"Good-bye!" was the answering cry, and then the visitors left in a crowd, waving their hands as they disappeared around a turn of the road.

"What a perfectly lovely time we have had!" declared Nan to Bert.

"Oh, the country can't be beat!" answered her twin brother. "Still, I'll be glad to get to the seashore, won't you?"

"Oh yes. I want to see Cousin Dorothy."

"And I want to see the big ocean," put in Freddie.

"I want to ride on one of the funny donkeys," lisped Flossie. "And I want to make a sand castle."

"Me too!" chimed in Freddie.

"Hurrah for the seashore!" cried Bert, throwing his cap into the air, and then all went into the house, to get ready for a trip they looked forward to with extreme pleasure. And let us say good-bye, hoping to meet the Bobbsey Twins again.

The End